VILLY SADNESS

A Novella by Rodney Nelson

with drawings by Trygve Olson

NEW RIVERS PRESS 1987

Copyright © 1987 by Rodney Nelson
Library of Congress Catalog Card Number: 86-63567
ISBN 0-89823-093-4
All rights reserved
Typesetting & Design: Peregrine Publications, Inc.

PREVIOUS BOOKS BY RODNEY NELSON:

POETRY: Oregon Scroll
    Vigil
    Red River Album
    The Popcorn Man
    Thor's Home

FICTION: The Boots Brevik Saga
    The Green God
    Home River

Villy Sadness has been published with the aid of grants from the First Bank System Foundation and the National Endowment for the Arts (with funds provided by the Congress of the United States).

New Rivers Press Books are distributed by:

  The Talman Company and Bookslinger
  150-5th Avenue   213 East 4th St.
  New York, NY 10011   St. Paul, MN 55101

Villy Sadness has been manufactured in the United States of America for New Rivers Press, Inc. (C. W. Truesdale, editor/publisher), 1602 Selby Ave., St. Paul, MN 55104 in a first edition of 1200 copies.

VILLY SADNESS

The news that Helmer Nelson has been shot is more upsetting than it should be. Nobody in Hedmark Township will mourn; I won't, though I knew him. I doubt that he had living relatives. Helmer was a *character* but not a village idiot whom people could look down on and accept. He had a way of making others feel unenlightened, so they shunned him. Myself, I regarded him as an inverted plains evangelist.

Word came at eleven last night, three hours after I had relieved Ben at the switchboard. A single protracted ring means *operator* and probably, at this time of the shift, trouble; but around Hedmark troubles tend to be slight.

Is it Villy?

Yes, Art.

This is Art talking. I suppose you'd better call the sheriff, because Helmer Nelson is dead.

Dead, you say. Where?

I heard the shot and went over, so now he's lying on the driveway to his place. I covered him with a tarp.

Was it like Erik?

No, and there's no gun.

My impulse was to ask whether Art had seen any footprints. It is the end of the main growing season and most of the fields have been plowed. I could picture all the dry black dirt. But, as Art would have said, you don't look for tracks in the middle of the night; so I let him hang up. I had mentioned Erik Rustad, the suicide, only to rid my mind of that picture. Helmer would not have killed himself.

Hedmark Township is an inward place where people are born, live, and die and keep the rest to themselves. Acts of human violence are usually self-inflicted (as with Erik), though evil exists; it must wherever people are. But here the gossip and the stealing and the mendacity seem somehow held in check, so that one has a chance of avoiding them without leaving. It's a good habitat for the aging bachelor or widower, else Erik Rustad and Helmer Nelson and my brother Ben and I would not have remained. When good or bad things happen—a church party, a fire—the man at the switchboard is told at once to tell others, and immediately, if the caller is on a township line, the others know. But as I talked to Art, I detected no rubbernecking; the farm wives were asleep. I could be alone with the news that something had happened which was both sad and strange.

Before he called I was thinking about Professor Henri Bergson, whose works I have yet to read. I'm always reading but not in philosophy, even though I'm always thinking too. I fear the side-effects. There is a difference between a thinker and a telephone tinker that has nothing to do with native intelligence; it's base livelihood. Today, the philosopher is attached to some academic institution where he *professes* for a living—in the two passages I saw, Bergson was titled *professor*—just like a theologian of old. The world expects him to voice his thoughts. But if a thinking telephone man were to try to do so, people would consider it not only unusual but unseemly. I'd agree with them. Younger, I used to open my mouth, talk science or music on the job, and the farmers of Hedmark Township would say *Is that right, professor?* My attitude was close to Helmer's in those days, and I resented what I took to be ignorance, especially when *I* had provoked an expression of it; but unlike Helmer I came to recognize the farmers' wisdom.

A reasoning man who devotes his life to telephony has chosen solitude. He may read and think as much as he pleases, but he should be careful: there is no one to watch him. The *professional* thinker acts within the limits of an institution, and thinking is his act. The thoughts of a telephone man can lead to mania.

This solitude rests on a balance which reading philosophy may upset, a balance between thinking and doing, and I've thought so long and so much that I've had to train my mind to hold back from other thinkers' words as it does from the lives around me. What I fear is the contagion of dogma. The unwalled institution of the prairie seems to invite extremism, luring a thinker on until he's wild for systematic restraint and has to become Catholic, Communist, or McCarthyite. Thus the side-effects of political thought on Helmer—and on Bob Rustad. I too might have been a bright rural doctrinaire.

I speak of Helmer as still living. He did have a place here, and his absence will be noticed if not regretted. It was due to one of his remarks that I was thinking about Professor Henri Bergson: *You know, the American forces did not participate in the fighting between the Allies and the Bolsheviks.* Helmer's style is—was—to begin with a statement apropos of nothing, or with a question like *Can you guess the population of Moscow in 1918?* That was just to get a person talking; notorious bores have to use a trick or two. I was passing him on the way home from the grocery store, the shady bench out in front where he and Doc Benson sat wasting the afternoon. Old Doc, being deaf now, was immune to Helmer.

The hell, I told him, not stopping. He waved a scrap of paper. No doubt he had read the remark to me.

You can look it up, he called. *It says right there in the Columbia Encyclopedia.*

I did as he suggested. He had in fact uncovered evidence that might expose me as a grandiose liar, that would for sure cast doubt on my story and also on my arguments of the last thirty years; no wonder he sounded so pleased with himself. I could say the encyclopedia was wrong and produce my own evidence, souvenirs and photographs and letters, as well as references in books (in *The Life of Woodrow Wilson*, for instance). However, to rebut Helmer is—was—to encourage him, and I didn't want to do that. He'd be waiting for an excuse to grunt *coverup* or *lies*, and the truth be hanged. I checked the life of Wilson merely for my own sake, and there it was, a note on Bergson's secret government mission to the United States, the object being to convince our president to intervene in north Russia. I must have seen the name before. This time, since I had the encyclopedia out, I thought I'd look under *Henri Bergson*.

So it was because of Helmer that I found a clue to the meaning of my work. A telephone man, even one who reads and thinks, may never get around to asking himself *why do I do this?* The life is too simple, too clean, too satisfying; no one else would be likely to question him on it either. This work afforded the invisibility and anonymity my hermit nature desired. Retreating to a forest hut would have been much more complicated. But that wasn't it. *Why*, I failed to ask, *do I love the presence of current?* My fingers have known the magic of telephony all along, delighting in their contact with the planet's pulse. Yet the words didn't begin to come until I saw a phrase which the encyclopedists had left untranslated, as though they too had sensed magic: *élan vital*. This is it— vital current, impulse, pulse. I let the words flicker and die down, sat at the quiet switchboard almost liking Helmer.

I was about to put my solitude into words, to express, finally, the balance of thinking and doing I have achieved. It is this balance the news has upset. Helmer dead is as upsetting as Helmer alive. As I talked to the sheriff *(he rented the farmstead one-half mile west of Hedmark, first one on your right—I guess he's lying on the road there—I don't know, you'll have to ask Mr. Engstrom at the next farm, another quarter-mile on your left—he didn't say)*, I felt not curious but annoyed, like the man I had probably gotten out of bed. Both the sheriff and I wanted to be rid of Helmer Nelson. He had a sixty mile midnight drive to look forward to, not to mention interrogations and paper work, and I was faced with hours of coffee drinking at the board. Some spoken transactions would have to be made through me—the sheriff's, the coroner's, the ambulance men's, the reporters'—-and I estimated that I wouldn't be able to close until one-thirty or two.

However, no one placed a call to Wahpeton, nor were there any incoming long distance calls. I heard only from Tina Engstrom, Art's wife. *Ya the sheriff made an arrest so they drove back right away, the ambulance and everything. It was Bob Rustad. I guess they were arguing about the Rosenbergs again. He shot him in the face. Ya I thought we'd better call you, Villy. God knows what else this year will bring.* Now I'd have some written word to leave Ben, who would be opening the switchboard at six-thirty. People would be asking him for information.

I slept well, rose in mid-morning, and as I ate I listened to my brother's magnificent contrabasso in the next room. The news was out; there'd be no rest for Ben. Since the *repair and service* sheet was blank I would have time to visit the farmstead—not that I was urgently interested. Leaving, I tried to catch his attention, but he was handling several calls and just managed to stare at me through lenses like bottle-bottoms.

Along that short stretch of gravel road Helmer had walked twice daily, into town in the forenoon, back at supper, and when seen from a distance, outlined against the abundant sky of the flatlands, he appeared motionless. But somehow, he'd advance, telephone pole to telephone pole, with knee-high buffalo grass (or snowbanks) lining the ditches beside him. There were trees at both ends of his route: to the east the larger grove, Hedmark, a steeple and roofs surmounting it; and westward the smaller, in which his bachelor home seemed hidden until he was almost to the driveway. I followed his evening path on wheels and at the wrong hour. Helmer would have been facing west in this light—and today he would have missed something superb. The late summer air is often dull with blown topsoil, thanks to plow and incessant winds; but now the souther had fallen.

I parked in his yard, not too near the house, and stepped into full clarity. The leaves of the surrounding elms and boxelders stood out in every detail, perhaps because at last they were not moving. Even the less sightly objects—the old frame house, the crooked barn, the abandoned implements—seemed more visible, hence more worthy of existence. It was hot, the air sweet with hay-smell, and it was silent but for the lilt of insects. Two red-tailed hawks swept close overhead, unfearing. I sensed that Helmer's death had liberated the place, that the removal of human restraint had allowed nature to return to itself; and I knew it was this missed moment one should live to experience. *This* was important, not what one *believes* or *professes*.

I hadn't come grieving anyway, nor was I set on entering the house, so I merely looked at the shiny silver padlock that hung through the doorhasp and read the sign. *No Trespassing by Order of Richland Cty. Sheriff Dept.* Ordinarily, in the case of violent death (though such a case is never ordinary in Hedmark Township), there is someone left in the home. Business continues. Or relatives take charge. Here, everything would be up to the law. The difference in Helmer's case was illustrated by the presence of the silver lock, and that in turn by what I saw as I peeked in at the kitchen window. No doubt the panes had last been washed in the time of old Mrs. Rustad; twenty years' bachelor smoke filmed them. A wooden chair and table were easy to make out in the dimness, also an ashtray and two stained cups. A stack of pamphlets lay there like food to be consumed, and it was harder to see the title of the one on top: *Come the Revolution.*

The Rustads had quit farming and bought a house in Fargo; that's where their children, including the murderer, were raised. It was the next year, 1933, after Rustad had given up trying to sell and decided to rent out the land and the farmstead separately, that Helmer asked me to connect the telephone. He would be the tenant, not Rustad's unmarried brother Erik, who was barbering and wanted to stay in town.

(Evidently, there was bound to be a violent death on this place. Last spring, in the barber shop, Erik mounted a chair, donned a noose, cut his left wrist with a razor, and jumped. It might well have happened here.)

That was to be my only visit to the farm till now, and one of the few times Helmer was to behave himself. He seemed almost polite as he let me in and poured me some ink-black coffee. Yes, he would like to have service restored. He thought the line was still functional. Rustad had taken the phone that belonged to the cooperative, but Helmer knew of a way to make the connection without added expense.

It's going to cost you to subscribe, I said, always prepared to dispute him.

Maybe so, but one cannot live isolated from the people. His tone was ingenuous and the look in his small blue eyes uncertain. Helmer was striving to say what he meant.

He went to the front room and carried in a box and set it gently on the table. I noticed that even his movements were hesitant. This was a stout, strong man who had worked most of his forty-three years as a seasonal laborer, for Rustad among others, and who retreated from no one. This was a mind capable of assimilating the doctrines of Christianity and Revolution, and forcing each aspect of his life to accord with what he believed, all the while going it alone in a place that was either indifferent or inimical towards his brand of prophecy. This was the man who stood in front of me like a timorous child offering a gift he hoped I wouldn't refuse.

Helmer had found an ancient magneto set, a relic of the beginnings of the telephone age, when farmers had organized to purchase and install their own equipment and hang their own lines, occasionally using barbed wire in a pinch. The days of heroism, ingenuity, and the closed rural system were gone, a fact Helmer should have known and, being *progressive*, hailed. I could tell he was aware of a gap in his vast self-education. He had allowed himself to treat me as an equal only because I represented technology. I wanted to laugh but chose to goad him.

No reason we couldn't hook this up, he said.

Hook it up and forget it, you mean.

Oh? Helmer compressed his thick lips. The masquerade was tiring.

This isn't 1910, Helmer, I lectured. *We have a common battery now, and outside lines. This thing belongs in the museum or in the dump. You should keep abreast of the times, Helmer.*

Well, I know that.

I popped open the box and displayed its near-empty interior. *See? This is where the galvanic unit sat, all the source of current you had. They don't even make batteries like that anymore. And here the line came in. Simply no way of connecting one of ours to it. But if you're serious about having a telephone, I can get you an apparatus that works.*

His sneer showed that the old Helmer was back. *I suppose*, he said, *you won't be happy until I'm giving all my money to A.T.&T.*

Bell doesn't own us. We have access to their long lines and crews and that's it. You'd be joining a modern cooperative.

I had strayed from character, spoken like the apostle of gadgetry I've never been, like the same rustic Edisons who in their machineshops had proved to be so impervious to the teachings of Helmer, and the great manipulator understood. He had the words to arrange a situation and control it, but in this instance the words had gotten out of hand. Helmer didn't indulge in personal animosity; it was too *bourgeois*. Yet, as he grabbed our coffee cups and took them away, I could feel it everywhere. There would be no refills.

It's all part of one big blood-sucking corporation, he said to the kitchen wall. *Now, if you don't mind, I have some studying to do.*

That was twenty years ago in Helmer's golden decade. He might have called me an idiot or a liar; he could afford to be bold then. But no, in his eyes I was simply another willing dupe of the plutocrats, an object to be saved rather than smitten. Anything *individual*, like my arrogance, didn't count. Helmer's piety was such that it survived the Hitler-Stalin pact and the Soviets' domination of eastern Europe after the war—the war itself, when America and Russia and Helmer Nelson were temporarily in alliance, had been an extension of his decade—and of course it remained unshaken through the Hiss trial, Korea, the Rosenbergs, and up to now, 1953, of which Tina has said *God knows what else this year will bring*. He did become more subdued after Korea, with Joe McCarthy on the ascendant. It wasn't *his* age showing.

Today's people are just that, people who belong to the day; this is because of their complete immersion in news. For a long time it used a visual inlet, the written word, but the daily paper seemed to exist outside of one—unlike radio, which brought it straight into one's ear. The telephone is an equally intimate medium; however, it permits transmitting as well as receiving and above all it is private. Radio made the news a Wagnerian sea of sound in which one could bob endlessly with the unseen millions. Once the contemporary experiences of the world had lost their remoteness, the listener could seem to share in them. The listener could be swayed: even the willing and unwilling dupes of Hedmark Township, North Dakota became passionately involved in the Truman-MacArthur scuffle. The Hedmark farmers have always had enough to do. Their susceptibility is no greater than say, Chicagoans'. It was during the war, when radio provided what was not only interesting but crucial, that news began to absorb *everybody*. This sense of living in the day grew to be pleasant, and one did not think of turning off the flow.

Helmer was a man of the word. In his sermonizing youth it had meant not simply language but the Word itself, and the essence of that remained in his oratorical prime. He sought gospel in news — I don't know how many papers he subscribed to; a dozen at least — and a pulpit in writing letters to the editor. The rest of his mission was talk. By the late 1930's he was debating all comers at the Hedmark Cafe and Tavern (all, that is, except lawyer Iverson and myself, the one nasty in argument and the other an unblinking enigma), spurred by his young admirer Paal, the owner's stepson, and if people did not take him too seriously, they did give him a chance to talk. His bait, the creating of a *popular front* against Hitler and Mussolini, was easy to swallow in 1939; also, he avoided discussing things that might have aroused hostility, like the tenets of his *belief*. The phrases he kept. One could speak glibly then of *the masses* and *the struggle*. Even writers in the national press were doing it. I remember his cleverness in dropping them at the instant the audience seemed ready to agree. *Peace is the condition America and the world proletariat aspire to*. During the depression, which was mental as well as economic, one yearned to say yea. Helmer induced the mood of assent. That, not his exact words, mattered.

I might have thought that in the postwar deluge of sound there would have been room for Helmer's voice. But the larger the chorus, the more pressing the need for harmony. Radio forbade now the dissonance of the 30's and after, and Helmer went silent. Not that he had lost faith — he just quit performing in person. His high-flown cafe speeches and arguments in front of the grocery store were ended, but he still wrote letters to *The Fargo Express* where they continued to appear. (The editor in Wahpeton stopped publishing him; what Helmer had called the Berlin airlift, *an unwarranted tampering with the self-*

determination of a sovereign people, had outraged certain backers of *The Richland News*.) So he had not given up. I could tell, as the tone of his letters became drier, statlier, that he had assessed the situation. He realized that for today his task was to provide a minor counterpoint to news, else his mission would not survive. Thus: not *the Alger Hiss frame-up shows unmistakable evidence of wrongdoing in government*, but *our nation is great enough to pardon Hiss for what he may or may not have done under stress of war, and send him home*; and not *the United Nations' imperialist designs on North Korea must be thwarted*, but *let us give our negotiators at Panmunjom every encouragement so that the peoples of both Koreas may once again enjoy peace and tranquility*. He walked to Hedmark as always. Indeed, he was oftener seen in town than in the fields. While there was much work to be done, the farmers had nothing for him. *He's getting too old*, some said; but everybody, Helmer included, got the meaning, He took to sharpening saws and knives in a shed behind the post office, and that earned him the little he required. But Helmer was not withdrawing from people; he had merely found a new role. It amused me to see him playing the mellowed philosopher—quiet, unassuming, pithy on occasion—and when I visited his saw-shop last March, I was not let down. He produced a bland smile out of nowhere, as though I were not an old antagonist intruding, but a friend.

Joe's dead, I told him.

The smile intensified. *McCarthy?*

No, Uncle.

The Helmer Nelson of 1953 was a version of what the long lost budding evangelist would have turned into, had not the century intervened. Or had that peculiar mind of his been wired differently. I'm thinking only of the surface Helmer, a neat, good-natured fellow at the edge of age, a familiar Hedmark sight. It wouldn't have surprised me to catch him with the Bible again. But I knew that the rapt, rabid Helmer was waiting to come out, and when it happened, amid the hysteria of the *world movement to save the Rosenbergs*, I sensed that he had miscalculated. I didn't pretend to understand it all, but I saw sources of danger he must have overlooked: one, television; two, the true feelings of *the people*. Reemerging in a series of letters to the Fargo paper, he abandoned his new role with fury. Helmer's was an uprising of the oppressed.

To the bosses and butchers who would murder these poor innocent people, I say beware. The masses will not stand by and see justice throttled. Everywhere in the world, in America, in France, in the Soviet Union, we are watching you and we recognize what you represent, and this is not democracy: it is Nazism. I say we shall not rest until you heed the demands of justice and common decency. Free the Rosenbergs!

I suspect that the editor of *The Fargo Express*, a man not known for his liberal sentiments, had reason to let Helmer in. Here was the perfect cartoon of a rural crank, *typifying*, as he wrote about someone else, *those who have made the traitors' cause their own*. He could depend on the McCarthyites to send rebuttals. Yet this letter of early June was to be Helmer's valediction.

I strolled around the yard. There are several abandoned farms in the township, and this had the cast of one that had been left ten years rather than a day ago. Helmer had lived in his own manner, hence the weeds were allowed to do the same. Dragonflies were busy in the still noon. It would be a good night for the bats. He had never owned a car, and the overgrown driveway seemed more like an untrodden cattle thoroughfare. Boot prints, his no doubt, marked the trail in the middle of it. The thick vegetation was trying to right itself where others' vehicles had passed. As I walked out of tree-shadow to the exposed junction of the township road, I savored the moment's windlessness, but I was also scanning the ground. *He's lying on the driveway to his place.* Where, though? They would have kicked dirt over any blood. Helmer had been shot after some *arguing about the Rosenbergs*, which must have occurred in Hedmark—if the two of them had argued here it probably would have been indoors. The bar stayed open late and served coffee as well; Helmer didn't drink. Once, on a night service call, I had spotted him going home. There had been an argument at the bar, I supposed, then Bob had followed him, lights off. In that case he most likely would have been hit just in from the junction, near enough the road so that Bob, lowering the car window—shouting his name?—would have had an easy target.

Everyone knew more than I. Had I wanted facts, I could have asked in town. But I preferred to remain ignorant awhile, to be alone at the site where Helmer had become news. My picture of the event seemed credible; there *was* a scuffed patch not far up the driveway. Dozens of shoe prints and crisscrossing tire tracks had effaced all sign of the man. But something of him was still here. I felt it in the place. It wasn't a ghost. Maybe it was what an abrupt death leaves instead.

Someone who's had schooling in violent death is able to understand its simplicity. What I learned as a young soldier has never changed. Such death is not an *it* but a seemingly random stroke that has little to do with the *enemy* or *murderer* against whom the reactions of the surviving are directed. The stroke just falls. A man lies on the road. The trees stand there, simply being themselves, and people do the same. They cannot word their emotion; there are no words. The sky just happens to be light—or low with rain. People know that the stroke was and would be inescapable, but they must move anyhow, deploy, track down the thing which delivered it; though perhaps they are really hoping to find and reclaim what it took away. Sure enough: in the mud they see the prints of a two-legged running creature.

However, I saw none in the black plowing to the east. While I couldn't imagine Bob on foot—Helmer's generation was the last to walk, and in the township he and O. H. Iverson and Lars Hedin were the last who actually did so—my military eye obeyed habit. The effect of education in battle is watchfulness. One can no longer accept anything; trusting in appearances has been shown to be fatal. Human testimony, like a spy's report, means to cover rather than state the truth. So one watches and listens. One lives on guard, though not necessarily in fear. Staying alert to deception makes reality plain. This is why I noticed things that Helmer, who lacked my makeshift wisdom, was blind to; and *God knows what else*.

With radio, the experiences of the world only seemed to become less remote. Today's people slid into a mass illusion, believing that events in Korea and New York were no less substantive than those right around them. A flat tire must be fixed and so must the Rosenbergs; both jobs appear to need personal attention. (I should say, appear to *demand*, and attention of the *same sort*; for news spellbinds one to an unending personal emergency.) Yet one's response to the flat will be modified by the sky, the hour, the condition of one's health and marriage, while there will be fewer mundane restraints on what one might do about the Rosenbergs. But rage, whether illusory in origin or not, of Bob's kind or Helmer's, must find a way of expressing itself. Changing tires can bust a knuckle and ruin a shirt, but at least it's a deed to counterpose the pique of the flat. Radio listeners in Hedmark Township, North Dakota could *do* nothing in answer to the Rosenberg case, hence their rage turned abstract. It was three weeks before that odd young couple were executed that I literally saw danger emerging. Television reached North Dakota. It was as though everyone had been waiting since the advent of the race; waiting for news of Noah or Abraham or the second coming, news promising deliverance from time. Television posed as the thing awaited. Look long enough, and the answer may appear. Ben and I were among the few who didn't purchase a set. His weak eyes and my love of the dark and silence limited us to older modes of waiting. Antennae were all over town, and the Hedmarkers began staying in the now public privacy of their homes. I remained where I had always liked to be, outside, off stage, beyond the audience; my link to the world, a wire.

Art Engstrom drove up and parked along the shoulder. He would have had the binoculars on me; nothing moves in Art's domain but he's aware of it. His is the next farm, and he has been renting the Rustad tillage from Bob. Thus Art and Helmer paid the same landlord. *You found the spot, Villy*, he said.

So this was it.

Ya it was a real mess last night, I can tell you. Some of the brains were shot out. Those sheriffs took most of it with, and they buried the rest.

Not the body.

Oh no, just what blew out. It was a shotgun, you know. I guess the coroner has the body.

We stood there and devoted a minute of silence to the memory of the event. Ditch-grass lay hot and unstirring in the midday sun. The bugs had retreated to shade, and all I could hear was the far piping of a tractor. While I could have done without the news Art was carrying, it would be just as well to get it from him. He was born in 1900 like myself, we went through school together, and he enlisted about when I did in the spring of '18. His regiment arrived in France just before the armistice—mine was already fighting in north Russia—so even if Art missed combat he was in on the doughboys' triumphal return. I was the last live war veteran to come home, and by the summer of '19 the flurry was over. People were tired of smiling. The Hedmarkers received me with a bit of suspicion; perhaps I had been in trouble. I soon learned, to my amazement, that the government had told them little or nothing of our Russian campaign. Few recognized the name of Arkhangelsk. It was then that the short, poker-faced Art Engstrom did me a service: he believed what I said. We hadn't been real friends.

I shunned the veterans' gatherings he attended. But somehow he made his understanding evident. In my young bitterness, I was ready to trust a man who didn't avoid my eye as he listened. I still trusted him. That's why I thought that he, if anyone, would have the news straight.

It was a terrible thing, in spite of how he was, said Art. *It was a terrible, terrible thing.*

They were arguing in town, you say?

Well, I left early, and it wasn't much going on then. It was Doc and Arvid and Helmer in the bar, and Bob. Bob was pretty drunk, though. I guess he really went after Helmer, but not violent. You don't hit an old guy like that. Helmer left, then he just waited and drove out after him. I guess in the bar they had no idea he was going to do a thing like this.

I suppose they arrested him here.

Ya he started drving back to Fargo, but he says he felt so bad that he came and turned himself in. Must have sobered up good and quick. Who would have thought that Bob—uffda.

You'll have to testify, and the others as well.

No way out of that. Nossir. Say, Ben wants you to make a pot of coffee. He's stuck at the switchboard, and he called Tina.

For Art Engstrom, too, the news is more upsetting than it should be. The shotgunning of Helmer just doesn't belong, *in spite of how he was.* Art got into his car, having told not quite all he thought, but having justified his trip by passing the message from Ben, and headed slowly west. The report of the Rosenberg argument must have originated with Arvid or Carl the bar-owner—Doc couldn't have heard—or someone who came in later, else Art, who'd had a beer with the principals, would have mentioned it. Perhaps Bob had used it in trying to extenuate his deed. Yet Art must have been here for the arrest and would have remembered more than the one indirect quotation: *he says he felt so bad.* He had discussed it with Tina, my informant, but not with me. Either Art preferred not to identify the source (he's no gossip) until the event had been morally digested, or he was scared, his tongue checked by a primitive fear that *any* reference to the Rosenbergs might bring back the stroke we're all awaiting. That's how upsetting the news could be.

I respect the farmers' pragmatic wisdom, but it won't help them now. They adjudge the world as experience in it, theirs and their ancestors', has taught them to; only murder, which hasn't happened since the time of settlement, is a thing neglected. It belongs to elsewhere, to news, and in their reponse to bloodlettings in Fargo or Minneapolis there is a tinge of disapproval—of not just murder but place. I'm as glad as they to be living in this snug, smug township, and my balance is also upset. But mine may be restored before theirs. I have a telescopic view which lets me pick out features in the surroundings of Bob's act. The farmers are too close to what I'm looking at to understand; they're part of the array.

I could tell them that murder is always thinkable, because where human beings are involved, anything can happen. Those who knew the worst of war, not only in the trenches but among the demoralized civilians, would at least be able to follow me: not Art, however. *Who would have thought that Bob* could kill a man? In fact, it is not unthinkable at all. He had done it to people wearing the Japanese army uniform, and I could say that the identity of the kill doesn't matter. The deed exists in a man's brain and emerges right at the point where his abstract anger becomes suddenly objectified. The aiming and the firing express the wish of the deed to return to abstraction. That he's acting in North Dakota rather than in the Pacific, and not in battle, means no more to him than the name of the thing he's trying to dematerialize. He is wholly gripped by the impersonal.

While humans are apt to do anything, I think *this* man was meant to serve *this* murder. Even in my state of unbalance I have been sure of his culpability. I wouldn't dare to tell the farmers, though; they'd get me for hindsight. Anyway, the real puzzle lies not in the event but in why it occurred here.

When a person leaves Hedmark, his reputation in the township stays exactly as it was at the time of departure. I went to war under the cognomen Villy Sadness, a happy ballplaying kid, and I was supposed to come back in every respect the same. That I was changed didn't fit, so they merely ignored Corporal William Sandness (who was now very sad indeed) and let joking Villy go on. It must have been a sinusitic old-timer's pronunciation that had stuck, and I didn't worry about the name until I was forced to bear it past my youth. It had been sitting here while I was overseas, and I was doomed to grow into it. Correcting people wouldn't work; they'd see me as affected. I had no choice but to be Villy Sadness. Older, I began to value my local cognomen. It reflected the place which had given it to me, and, for someone who wants to be left alone, there's no better shield than a mirror.

The township may have been more or less right about Villy, but it didn't have a chance to prepare a reputation for Bob Rustad. He left Hedmark in childhood, when a person doesn't own his name but shares it, like bed and board, with the family. Thinking back to the year they moved, I can't even remember Bob; only the Rustads. They were not a large clan, nor had they done much since settlement days to earn esteem. Their farm looked seedy and their fields ragged. Jens had surrendered to the depression earlier than anybody, taken the Mrs. and their few kids and things on a one-way trip to Fargo, and he hardly ever revisited the neighborhood. Erik was the last Rustad here. Thus Bob, along with his siblings, remained frozen in anonymity. People might hear that he had graduated from Central High and joined the Marines and seen action in the Pacific and come home to marry a Fargo girl, but where Hedmark Township was concerned, he would always be one of *that Rustad bunch*, whose minor follies were to include Erik's suicide.

So it stood until both Jens and the Mrs. died in 1950. Bob either inherited the whole farm or bought out his siblings. Nobody, not even Art, who used to deliver his rent in person and had seen a little of the family, knew the exact arrangement; just that Bob had become landlord. I heard that he was appearing, as drinker and teller of war stories, at Carl's once in a while. But the *he* people spoke of was not, to their minds, any known individual. The forerunning child would always be faceless. *He* was simply another strange man in town, someone who happened to have a name that was receding into the history of the neighborhood (where it would be given passing notice) but represented the outside. He must have been heir to his uncle as well. I ran into him on the morning after Erik's big jump. He had carried a sack of rags and a bucket out of the shop and was locking the door. When he nodded and said *Hello, Villy*, I realized the extent to which I had figured in his early world: a kid knows us if we don't know him. His smile, a veteran's, implied that since I too had dealt in blood, I wouldn't expect him to be sorrowing. *Well, I cleaned most of the mess*, he said. *All I have to do now is get somebody to take it and pay the rent. From what I've seen, that's not easy.*

Missing the hint, I told him that I was sorry about his uncle. I didn't add that Erik, a glow in his voice, had been talking suicide forever, The town was calm that morning, as though in relief at Erik's triumph. Not that Bob would have cared; he'd have heard it all. He waited impatiently—a strong-looking, thirtyish man with a military haircut and an iron smile—until my condolences were over. Then he was putting the bucket and the stained rags in the trunk of the car (a new one) and racing off. What I missed was a hint that things were wrong between Helmer and Bob.

I lingered a moment at the barber shop. However, I couldn't feel its aura. Perhaps the stroke, when so eagerly invited, drops with reluctance and does not trouble the atmosphere. Perhaps it had come to Erik as it falls on the beds of the very old—as a stroke of the loving kind. There wasn't much discussion in the township. What could one say? *Ya so at last he did it*, and that was that. People were more interested in the visits of Bob Rustad, who, except for that morning I'd spoken with him, was not to be seen sober. *I guess he's in insurance*, said Carl, *and he seems to do all right. A regular booze-fighter, that guy.*

They were arguing about the Rosenbergs, but I had heard there was a further subject of contention. A fellow who has grown up poor is often obsessive about money, and I can see that with Bob Rustad it might have become both the token and the test of all human dealings. That Helmer, his opposite in this and every regard, should have been tied to Bob as a tenant was almost unnatural; and his delinquency in that role was more than enough to trip him. If he had saved a little through the years, it must have been just that. No doubt the sharpening business paid for his coffee and the doughnuts he made and the tobacco he never smoked in town. Subscriptions were perhaps his one luxury. It was about a month ago that Arvid told me of a scene in the barroom. Bob had gotten stuck on the topic of *those Jewish Reds*, whose death he was still celebrating, Helmer and Doc were buried in rummy, and everyone else was pretending to watch television. *But he wouldn't let go of it, he keeps saying they should have gotten the friends of the Rosenbergs while they were at it, like certain parties he won't name, he says. But that Helmer, he looks at his cards, and doesn't hear a thing. So finally, Bob gets mad and says if certain parties don't pay their rent he's going to kick them out and they can go and live in Soviet Russia and see how they like that.* None of us had succeeded in angering Helmer. This did it: in Hedmark Township, a man's finances are not publicly discussed. Yet Helmer was not so simple as to try to take a stand where there was no footing. He sidestepped the matter of the rent. *I never saw him white in the face like that, by golly, and I sure thought he was going to do something—at the age sixty-three or whatever he is. But when he talks it's just as cool as a cucumber, and he eyes Bob and he says, Those who want to play judge should look at themselves and their own people first.* Bob walked out cold. He was not too drunk to remember that night.

Since he rarely mentioned his wife and children or his business in Fargo, one had to deal with the Bob Rustad he himself portrayed: war veteran, American Legionnaire, anticommunist, man of the world. Who knew what the mask hid, or cared to find out? I'm as ignorant as any of his intimate life, but still I have an idea that Bob Rustad came to Hedmark not just to spurt verbal gas but in pursuit of a farm-dream. Those ten shaping years that ended in depression at the Rustad place were hard, yet he would have retained a picture of them, a green country picture set against the times' darkness; and the locale where the boy first saw it would continue to allure the man. In this instance, however, the man was so long torn from it that when at last he inherited the place, he had forgotten the directions. The city had matured him, and war, and it's more than twenty miles between Fargo and the past. Bob would have blamed his uprooting on others—the alcoholic is an incessant blamer—without considering that old Jens Rustad, like everyone in the 30's, was only doing his best. I think Bob's visits to Hedmark were not a groping homeward; he is too impercipient to try for synthesis. They meant he had resigned his claim to the country, but not in the least to justice. He wanted revenge. Unhappy Helmer was sitting right in his way, a person whom every article of his *faith* denounced, sitting, moreover, in the same green scene the world had robbed him of.

Thoughts of Bob and Helmer had worn me out as I walked in the yard of that green place, and now I was resting on the steps by the locked door. The elms west of the house are tall. Already their shade enclosed me. I watched the dragonflies hover and weave and dip, the hawk pair circling towards town, the kindle of midafternoon light in some near cottonwood trees, and I did not want to go. I've had it many times, a wish to loaf in the lap of nature, being instead of doing, yet I've never come up with a way to stay. Maybe it's part of a universal farm-dream that is not supposed to be substantiated, a vestige of what all creatures once enjoyed and were destined to lose; all young things must fly. But maybe it's more. Whether one is a bird or an insect or a man, one can always reconstruct the dream in maturity (or sometimes; mine would not take shape as a nest of my own). I find in my urge to be isolated in nature the inklings of a deeper, wiser life that I could, if I chose, make real. Humans tend to abuse the non-human, but there's a certain element nature receives only from us: the contemplative. I'd add it to the green scene of my withdrawal and thus assume my rightful place in being. However, as I waited in the undreamlike, non-human beauty of the Rustad farm, I knew that the arguments for going were still there. It was not that Ben needed me. His message had been coded. Fix him a pot of coffee meant that I should come around and chat this afternoon—Ben's too discreet—but it was nothing pressing; and I didn't have to guess what about. Nor was it the pull of the life I *have* chosen, which is almost a hermit's anyway. On the contrary, I was feeling oppressed by the world I'd gotten myself into, my circumscribed existence in an area that was not so remote from general violence and meaninglessness as I had imagined. A gunshot had brought the times to Hedmark Township, or revealed their presence, and where did I belong? I would leave these bruised wooden steps and go, but more reluctantly than ever. Living was the oppression, not death; and I'd go only because I realized that I had not yet borne enough of it and wasn't ready. One should not stop action until one is prepared to face an upwelling of thoughts which the act of living has kept down. I wasn't ready, so I went to my truck and quit silence.

Between Hedmark and the Rustads', the federal highway crosses the township road, and on the treeless southwest corner of the intersection is an ugly house which Al Klocke, whose father owns that land, built and moved into last year. It is a pink, shedlike building set in a vast lawn of dirt, or, when it rains, gumbo. The grass he planted is trying, as are the runt poplars and Chinese elms which in time are supposed to block the west wind—never mind the south or the north. I think it's since the storm in June that a tricycle has been stuck in the yard, only the seat and the handlebars showing. It was then too that Al made a causeway of planks so that he could get from the road (where he had to park) to the stranded house. When the mud became dirt, both trike and the causeway remained: mementos of trouble. I have not been able to understand why he did not build on one of his father's well-treed vacant properties or on the Klocke farm itself, where there would have been room for a second house. Al would have had immediate lawn and shelter, not to mention an attractive setting; but he preferred to live in the open, like a rodent too dumb to dig, in a country the sky rules. If Al *were* stupid, he'd be less of an enigma. As it is, he's a nice, intelligent young fellow who never left the farm, married a local girl, and went into partnership with his dad. He grew up in the old Klocke house, one of those proud structures the early men designed so artfully, and as a boy he helped in the tulip garden. I've had to think that Al is simply blind to all the immigrants saw and therefore typical of an age that cannot see what *is* but watches television. Yet when I drove by his pink monstrosity this afternoon— now it has an antenna—I was remembering in detail the day in '18 that I said goodbye to Hedmark and headed east, walking backwards mostly, to catch the train on the Minnesota side, at Nora, for the war; and the memory of that light instant in which I promised to return to the place I thought I hated, the sunshine clear, windless like today, carried along a whiff of the spirit I had then felt and which had driven the settlers of the prairie, and suddenly I understood Al Klocke. Coming to the stop sign, I arrived at another sort of intersection.

    May 17th it was, *syttende Mai*; an important date in the valley of the Red. Homesteading was only a few decades back, and the Norwegians, whose luggage had included old world patriotism, were celebrating their national holiday even though the war-whetted patriotism of the new disapproved of such *un-American* observances. Flags of Norway and the United States crowded the inside of Hedmark's one church (a Lutheran, of course), but the stars and stripes hung alone outside to appease any government agents in the neighborhood. The folks were living then, so I would go to services occasionally, however much I loathed those dour *norsk* preachings. I had no escape that day: whenever a young Hedmarker joined up, the Reverend Tiseth would announce and laud the event. As I suffered in the pew, breathing the cologne- and sweat-laden air and eager to be away, I took comfort in knowing that English sermons were short. War had banned longiloquence from the Hedmark pulpit at least: denied use of his native tongue, Tiseth had resorted to brevity. It was also *syttende Mai*, and a special time in which to receive honor, and the folks had made sure I'd attend. *Vun more gallant son af ar community iss to yoin da holy crussade*, the Reverend was concluding, his broad white face a map of struggle, *end sso naw vill Misster Villyum Ssandnesss ppleasse riisse*. I did, smiling. The whole congregation looked at me without moving their necks, Tiseth hissed a blessing, and the pump-organ ushered us out to the scent and color of spring's first warmth.

While nothing more had been planned, people seemed in no rush to take to their cars and buggies. They waited around in the bright church grass as at a reception that shouldn't be ended. It was indeed a special time, and not just Mr. William Sandness's: a twin apotheosis of holiday and spring imbued them all with what I'd now recognize as love. Vicariously, I was prince of it, and both the Reverend and I had to circulate to shake hands and greet them. *Ya Villy, you be careful — over there*, said Ola Engstrom, who had put Art on the train a week earlier. He was grinning, so I whistled a bar of the song he had cited. Everyone seemed as young and wise and unafraid as my coltish self, and I prattled without concern for the truth. Yes, I would be in the engineers— *right on the western front. They're going to train me in England.* The Hedmarkers entered into the game, their ooohs and aaahs crowning Villy a hero on the spot. People always like to send a kid to war; his absence will defend them. But it wasn't only compliments that made me feel like a winning pitcher, it was the day's heart-warmth embracing everyone. They didn't even mind Helmer who stood at the edge in an unbrushed suit, his thick hair watered down, trying to pass out leaflets on which he had typed antiwar quotations from the Bible. *Our Lord was a man of peace*, he murmured. *Do you know what He says about fighting? Here, just read it.* These sentiments, once popular in the township, had recently cost him his Sunday school job. It had been fine to talk peace and *damn that European quarrel*—until America got into it; then Helmer's pious consistency became unwelcome in the church basement. (He'd also had to forsake the upstairs.) But his dedication was such that he would appear after services to remind God's lambs of their straying, as he did my last innocent time in Hedmark, and I can still see his prim, ignored face and the sky reflected in his wire-rimmed glasses, his awkward steppings forth and back— what a portrait. In 1918 Helmer would have been twenty-eight or so, the son of a depot agent who had lived but a couple of years in town, where Helmer had finished school and chosen to stay. He was from Minneapolis, a city-born Norwegian like Ben and me. While we had arrived in Hedmark as children, Helmer had come at the end of most of his growing up and hence was to remain outside the social establishment that barely accepted us. No unmarried seasonal farm worker and handyman had much chance of breaking in, but he seemed comfortable in his lack of status anyhow, and his religious mania made him an unthreatening, if silly, *character*. To me he was that but an adult also; I had not yet qualified to needle him. *Well, I'm going to slay the Hun*, I said, putting on a small show of regret, *to slay or be slain, I guess*.

I saw anger in his squint and almost wished I hadn't spoken. *Is that what you want, Villy? Blood on your hands and your conscience? You want to live with that, do you?* The leaflets were trembling; however, Helmer had kept his voice down.

Many have no choice but to go, I told him, lost for a better reply, not meaning to insinuate that those who had gotten out of it would do well to mind their righteousness — Ben's vision was as poor as his — and hoping only to escape. I did not understand the risks of being nice to a pariah. One half-sympathetic word will tap a vat of unsaid emotion. Above all, I didn't care what Helmer thought of me or anything, not on a day that belonged so wholly to the sun-swept distances I was about to reach and when I could see, among the smiles of the crowd, someone who *did* embody the world I felt.

Whether he had missed my unconscious barb or not, Helmer turned soft and persuasive. *The Bible, it says thou shalt not kill, and there's no two ways about it. It's not too late to change your mind, Villy. You take this here and read and think it over*. I recall neither the look of the sheet nor the quotations on it, just that it existed in my hand before it passed to memory. I must have dropped it unread.

As I stopped at Klocke's intersection, I was not expecting my mental reassembly of that *syttende Mai* to lead to her. Time has taught me to leave certain times alone and sealed away from the rest of the material of remembering; what does not serve the *élan vital* must be immured. If I have thought of those times, it has been only of their vestiges. I have touched the protective scar tissue but not kneaded it. Yet this glimpse of Ingeborg, arm in arm with Tina on the shiny church steps, was not ringed in pain. It came as gladly to my eyes this afternoon as it did when I saw and approached her: a woman in her spring. It too had been closed in my mind, and longer than the late, hurtful remembrances. A widower's vanished fair times are the more difficult to think of. The two girls were watching me, Tina Boe and Ingeborg Revland, the two prettiest in the township, and when I got to the steps I didn't know what to say. But a military hero does not retreat. All those years that I had sat next to Ingeborg in school, I had dreamed of marrying the black-haired Tina, and then in our last month, as the windows let in April, I had begun noticing the slim ash-blonde beside me. It was her I looked at now, her amused green eyes and full lips, her hair coiled in a bun, her long white dress matching the walls of the church, and she looked back in easier silence than mine. There had been no courting, nothing done or said, only an exchange of glances. Tina had seemed unaware of her rejection; in fact, she had nursed our inchoate love by passing bits of news that were not quite messages. *I'm going to Revlands' to help them make butter*, she'd say to me in the post office (and then she'd tell Ingeborg, *I saw Villy in town today*—I was to learn of everything). Our shy, preverbal conversation at the church went on until the good Tina broke it. *So when are you off, Villy?*

I take the three o'clock train.

No, so soon? Weren't you leaving next week? Tina's real or fabricated sorrow caused Ingeborg and me to turn to her. Besides, she was speaking for both of us.

I'm going to pack all my troubles in an old kit bag, I said, trying to josh but somehow unable to, *and I'll be tenting tonight on the old camp ground.*

Not tonight! said Tina.

Well, after I get to the front.

When Ingeborg shook my hand, her smile was direct. I saw no apprehension in it, and there was none in her voice either: *Good luck to you, Villy.*

My ears were hot as I mumbled thanks, I'd be seeing them. I had a long, long trail awinding, but I must have felt as sure as Ingeborg that I'd return. Having convinced Ma and Pa and Ben not to drive me to the depot—*I need to train my legs*, I had argued—I began my happy, often backwards march on the three-mile road to Nora. I strode through the towering clear light of the prairie and whistled to the applause of meadowlarks and red-winged blackbirds. Tomorrow beckoned in the slowly opening riverwoods that marked its frontier; at last I'd be crossing. But the place I wanted to lose held on, kept drawing my eyes west, and I stopped at the bridge to look it into limbo. The words on my tongue belied what I was experiencing. All I could say to the dwindled outline of Hedmark was *adieu and to hell with you*, for I was shucking the pettiness of childhood and did not know that I had already become a man that *syttende Mai*. Yet it was this moment that was to be imaged and endure. In the land I saw it is always two o'clock on a perfect spring afternoon and life is always new, the work always beginning, and there is always one more stretch of virgin sod to plow. *Guess I'll be back sometime*, I remember thinking, and I laughed as I walked on towards Nora. The experience had set, however. When I got out of the army, I might have lived anywhere I chose, and I was to return in search of this moment; perhaps some deity had given the image so that I would. The right words for it were not discovered till the intersection. I had seen the west of the pioneers.

Whether I contemplate it now or through the eyes of this afternoon or of thirty-five years ago, the scene itself remains fixed—not so much outside as above time. Change is evident only in the words that have accumulated in the viewer to enlarge the dimensions of understanding. The vivid sky, the earth-scented air, the bird-voices, the fields on fields of immature wheat, the tiny steeple midmost in the horizon, all its details exist in a consonance that brings the word *joy* to mind. Beethoven's *Freude* would be truer, or *joie de vivre*; the setting has more hope and love in it than our poor *joy* conveys. The experience of it is not just mine. I share it with the numberless men who transmuted a dream into this hemisphere, so I must call it, as they did and their sons do, the west. Al Klocke's move to a naked acre when he might have built in a soft green one is not a rejection of beauty but a quitting of his bondage to the past, and his achievement of a new life on new land is an inspired, if scrubby, reenacting of the pioneer drama. I waited at the stop sign until I could see in a pink shed and a kid's half-buried tricycle the casual residuum of the same west I had felt in 1918 and which, to my *joie*, was to welcome me back a year later in an exact gemination of the day I had walked to the depot. The same Ingeborg was to be there too, at church and dressed for Sunday—the young Ingeborg who had spirited the scene of my departure and whose image I had put out of mind to save myself. Yet she had released the west. It could not have appeared today without her. I crossed the intersection slowly, knowing the ban was gone, but still afraid.

Afternoons in Hedmark are never bustling and now, with the kids in school, it looked like a well-kept cemetery. The streets lay broad and vacant, their dust unstirred, and walls of inert leaf enclosed the tombstone-white of the houses. Some farmer was driving his grain-truck into the elevator, and there was but one vehicle, O. H. Iverson's '39 Ford, parked uptown. The only living thing in sight was Carl's retired three-legged dog hobbling towards the better shade of the post office. It used to be an active place. Horses and cars and buggies would teem in the main street at almost any hour of day or evening. Depression put an end to its rise. But I wouldn't say that Hedmark is a dying town. The majority of those who were to move away did so before the end of the war, and since that time six people have come in or been born every year and six have left or died. Hedmark is static. I know that at least one of its 272 inhabitants would like it to maintain such a balance. The sight of O. H. Iverson in the business door of the post office reminded me that the balance is off. He had spotted my truck and would be ready to continue what bombast he'd been directing at the postmaster. I saw him watching, a stocky old man in a moustache and a crooked panama hat, as I approached on the baking sidewalk: O. H. Iverson, lawyer, politico, scapegrace, and scourge.

You knaw, Villy, he said, his tone reflective at this point, *ve live in an age of mechanical inventions. There are some vhich are good. That truck of yours—vithout that truck you vouldn't be able to get out and do your vork. Then there are some vhich are no good, like a par-mor. You don't need an engine on a mor to cut grass. Man vas made to sving a scythe, you knaw. Vell the telephone, that vas a good invention, and in spite of vhat the vomenfolks do vith it, and I can tell you vhy.* Here O. H. began turning up his volume. I nodded and listened. The flattery was meant to beguile. Any said response would have been premature. *Because the telephone reduces the risks of living alone in the country. In olden times, if something vent wrong on the farm, there vas no vay to get help in a hurry and you could just lie there and bleed to death. But now all you got to do is pick up and call the ambulance or the sheriff or the man down the road and that's it. Everybody in his right mind should have a telephone.* O. H. paused to glare me in the eye. The conclusion would be next. *If there had been a telephone out at Helmer Nelson he might be living today, but Helmer Nelson had nothing but nonsense in his head. Let me tell you, Villy, it vas his own damn fault vhat happened!*

I think you may be right, I hastened to say, knowing that he wouldn't give me long. *Just look at Erik Rustad. He was certainly to blame for what happened to him, and he didn't have a telephone either.*

O. H. loosed the snort of a man who has been stranded too many years on Lilliput. Every telling point he made would be missed, but in despair, he'd keep trying. We know each other and are bound to say and do what's expected; thus it is my social duty to quip at his tirades. He likes me, though, and O. H. is one of the few *characters* whose presence I can tolerate. He may be dogmatic in his scolding of humankind, yet he's utterly without dogma—the *faithful*, Helmer and the late Reverend Tiseth, used to avoid him—and relies on written history for support. A law degree and a wide experience of books and the world make him an educated man, and he's let nobody forget it; as a result, he has never been elected to public office. Nor has his candid tongue brought in much revenue. People want a lawyer to be avaricious like themselves, not upright and arrogant, and O. H. has been wearing the same grey coat since 1920. When I see his soiled proud personage, I think he must be right, we *do* hate truth—he's its walking symbol. I respect O. H. in that he seeks the truth (if he rarely gets it whole), and even in his crank talk today there were glints of it. Yes, had there been a telephone at the house, Helmer might be living. To have installed a phone, he would have had to be different, but Helmer was what he was and full of *nonsense* and ergo he's dead. Here the argument begins to mystify, and I can only joke, *look at Erik Rustad*. Perhaps O. H. is indeed a savant and able to pick out connections I miss.

Erik vanted to die and he knew it, he went on doggedly. *Helmer Nelson vanted to die and he didn't know it. That's the distinction betveen a victim of suicide and a victim of homicide.*

I intended to see my brother and be off again, so, as we of Lilliput always do, it seems, I left the giant in the midst of his ponderings. It is not easy to take leave of O. H. Somehow, one does not wish to be rude to the man who may have just called one an ass.

The outdoor stairway on the side of the post office took me to the second floor, where Ben and I and the switchboard live. Dad purchased the building from Uncle Ted in 1906. It was a hotel then; Ted had constructed it in the days of the Territory and he ran it until he got the urge to homestead in northeast Montana. I don't remember Milwaukee, my birthplace, just a snatch of the end of our moving trip to the flatland. *Where are the trees*? I asked Ma, and her laugh was puzzling. The Sandnesses had been tradespeople even in the old country, city Norwegians unlike the rural-bred immigrants of Hedmark Township, and I think Ma came of town stock as well. Our time in

Milwaukee, where Dad part-owned a harness shop, was one of quick americanization; Ben and I couldn't talk the *norsk* one had to know to get along with the Hedmarkers, nor were we versed in farm ways. Growing up odd may have prepared me for my eccentric vocation. Yet this has been home—this landscape, this town, this building. The folks would have continued running the hotel, also the phone exchange, which Dad took on when the original co-op went broke, had the postwar influenza epidemic spared them. Both died while I was shipping out of north Russia, so I didn't hear of it till the day I marched west into a west that seemed purely bright. Good Ben, innocent of death as I'd been seeing it, sat here alone and full of responsibility. We didn't speak of Dad and Ma. All Ben's emotion was narrowed to *keep the business going*; he would express his grief through loyalty to what they had begun. Myself, I wanted to help my brother, and this was to bind me too to the covenant. We closed the hotel desk and moved our household and switchboard upstairs in 1933, leasing the ground floor to a tenant who has proved more reliable than one of Bob Rustad's: the United States of America. Ben didn't leave or marry, and he is the folks' true loyal son. I, twice renegade, have only the semblance.

The inside air was thick with new-brewed coffee, and I wasn't surprised to find him on the club sofa listening to the radio. Our *Hedmark Telephone Cooperative* occupies a large room over the street; the sofa is handy when the switchboard's idle. As *operator*, I've done a lot of reading. Poor Ben must get his words by ear.

He heard me turn off the set. *Villy?*

Ya.

The dimness I entered—the shades are always pulled—was like that of a sickroom, but his deep voice was no invalid's. It seemed to challenge the walls of his cramped domain, and it ruled what little space he had. Girls have fallen in love with the manly sound of him. Ben sat up and aimed his goggles at the blur that would be I.

Well, any news? I said, stealing his question.

He veiled his disappointment in a shrug. *I know as much as you, probably. I talked with Tina and some others have called, but seems nobody's heard a thing. They took Bob Rustad to the county jail, so I suppose he'll be tried in Wahpeton. I never met the guy. Doc and Arvid were the ones who were there, and maybe they could explain it—Carl too. But he's not answering the phone. Did you talk to him?*

No, just Art and old man Iverson.

There's been too much drinking, that's all I can say.

My chats with Ben are episodes in a continuing monologue of two; even the intervals are part of it. I don't believe we've ever had a real discussion or confessed to each other. Once I began to tell him my great war story and he looked so uncomfortable that I stopped and didn't resume. There's been not a mention of his own brave tale — the courtship of freckle-faced, black-haired Tina, which ended dismally when Private Art Engstrom came home. And I haven't asked. Though she kept Art a secret, Ben may feel he did wrong in chasing a soldier's girl. After my months with Ingeborg, *I* needed to be silent, and he let me heal. Trite objectivity has marked our monologue as it has our long shared life. Two such opposite partners, blood kin or not, have to preserve some distance. We were unalike from the beginning — I the tease and comedian, Ben the dark moralist; I tall and skinny, he squat and strong, blessed with the build of a rhinocerous (*and the eyesight, and the insight*! I used to taunt him, prancing around him like a mad young giraffe and dodging the next well-earned blow). He could handle his kid brother easily. It wasn't until high school, where he studied books and I used a bat, the two of us dreaming separately of Tina, that amity was reached. How he saw me then or in the '20's and how he sees me now, I don't know. Ben is mysterious by trade. Perhaps he too conducts a hidden monologue, weaves words as I've been doing and judges me equally strange. I still won't ask. Things unsaid to another may exist, but they do not threaten. To say it all is at times the same as shooting.

But I think he's had one cause to hate me. It was on Christmas Eve, 1921, the first sans Ingeborg, that Tina brought an apple pie. I haven't forgotten the sight of her in the entryway, so damned pink and smiling and married, or my choked gratitude. I had lost a wife and she a best friend; Tina gave not only a Christmas present but a memorial. There was a chill in the month and the heart, yet Ingeborg seemed to live again in the warmth of the pie. Ben must have understood. However, I could read the feeling in him before he turned and left the courtesies to my tied tongue. I had been successful in love, not he, and my loss meant less than the arrival at *my* door of the girl he had failed to win and who was now related to me, not him, through Ingeborg. The shame enjoining his anger would have come out hatred, and I know it's rankled him down the years. Tina made the pie an annual tradition but he's never accepted a slice of the gift, pretending a distaste for apples — which I know he loved. Things unasked do not threaten.

I sense it in him at Christmas, not the rest of the time. He probably bears himself more ill will than he does me and is able to master the feeling once the pie plate is gone. *I talked with Tina*, he can say. My brother is good and a man of *faith* but no evangelist. What he believes shows solely in the doing and the non-doing, and I've yet to see him violate the golden rule. His life is a postscript to the folks' catechism: not smoking, not drinking, not cursing (not even at his own purblindness), not fornicating. Ben has a record of non-deeds to match his hard work, honest practice, charity and church-going. He imposes on me to escort him to Sunday services and back — I don't have to go in — and this allows him to put up with my occasional brandy or cigar. If he has an unkind word, it's for a vice and not a person (*there's been too much drinking*); but Ben is not all saint. An imp emerges when he plays music, leers out of his usually sober face, and he heaves the accordion to and fro, swaying and sweating as he stomps to the beat. I once heard a recording of Gounod's *Faust*, and I think Ben's dance-band singing voice is as mephistophelean as Pinza's. It's surely no weaker; I wish Dad had let him take lessons. Staying in Hedmark Township, he had few opportunities to perform — only weddings, funerals, and the like required serious music — and Ben, or his imp, decided on popular entertainment. He's sung and played with a number of groups and appeared at old-time dances all over the county. His fellow bandmen provide him eyes and a ride, so I, thank the Lord, have not had to travel the schottische circuit. The music I'd want to hear would be symphonies and opera, and perhaps in time the local radio stations will share my taste; until then I must catch the odd recital in Fargo and sit home rereading my *Concert Companion*. I'm glad for Ben, though. His is a pinched life, and the dances have given vent to the mystery in him. Now that the old-timers are dying or danced out and the barns and the band-stands quieting, his imp will have to find new romping ground and I can't imagine where it'll be.

He palmed his hair. Ben's still dark at fifty-six; my own fair thatch has been greying. A sheltered existence has kept him young-looking and I think he's a little vain about it. The voice which makes him sound *just like a Hollywood star*, as the girls say, is an extra cause for vanity, and had he been less moral he would have flirted at the switchboard and become a Hedmark *character*. Ben is impervious to temptation from within and without. The two or three females who tried to besiege him—they didn't live in the township and perhaps had seen him perform and were misled—gave up when they realized how hopelessly content and self-contained he was. I doubt that even the shooting could have unbalanced my brother.

I suppose old O. H. didn't know anything either, he said as though thinking aloud. *He wouldn't get involved in a criminal case. They'll have to get somebody else to defend Bob Rustad.*

I wonder if they notified the relatives.

Ben probed the room until he located me again. *Helmer was born in Minneapolis, wasn't he? It's no use checking there, though, not with a name like Nelson. Maybe when they read through his things they'll find an address. Say, you can get yourself a cup.*

I'm going to Nora to see about a new front tire. I was lying. Ben nodded and said he would keep the pot on the stove, and I left him to examine the case in his way as I had been doing in mine. He too may understand by now that the significance of the murder lies not in its fact or history but in what it has stirred loose, and unlike me may have chosen to stick to its pidddling phenomenal aspects. Investigating the pit of oneself is hard.

I've heard that seers of the Orient, before they go to sleep, trace the acts and thoughts of the finished day in reverse, cultivating thereby the self-awareness that leads to enlightenment. I didn't lie down to practice their discipline; I only wanted to rest and forget. But the day has not ceased. Its chapters pass and pass before the mind and in an order that now seems not imposed but natural. The last-written page of my mental manuscript *is* the one on top, and I must work to establish a chronology. Why not tell the story as it is—at the moment of telling, the telling moment? Perhaps because the last-written is not the first-lived, and narrative's an attempt to imitate the clockwise flow of animal experience. Language represents mortality. The seers turn time's tale backwards to show that experience is not all. My late afternoon was spent traveling ground I had already crossed in thought, and in the light of the present my drive east on the road I'd been mentally occupying since the intersection seems like a pathetic acting out. Yet I had to *do* as well as think; the mind won't let reality come full until an action dares it. I headed not for Nora but a place I wasn't quite prepared to identify. If I'd said its name to someone, *Lindgrens'*, or even to myself, its every secret association would not have been imparted. Thus far have I withdrawn to the local nomenclature in which

Lindgrens' means just one more empty farmstead. Still, I don't say it. The conscious, worded plan involved revisiting trees and grass; I wanted to prolong the country solitude I'd only begun to enjoy at Rustads'. It was such an enticing prospect and the day so high and rife in the west that my mood covered my apprehensions.

Two drives meet at the road where it comes to the top of the riverbank. The one north leads to Pete Johannesson's, a big shady farm that has been lived on and manicured since the morning of settlement. I took the other, an unused pair of ruts winding south along the bank a quarter mile to Lindgrens', but I stopped a short ways in. The western drop to the Red is considerable, at least for around here; it's almost like a bluff. When one's approaching from Hedmark, the superstructure of the Nora bridge awaits at eye level. Yet the grade is gentle enough to let the grass thrive and old boys of the neighborhood sit and fish and reap the sun, which also prospers in this lone break in the riverwoods. It is the only park, albeit undedicated and unmaintained, in the entire township. I've seen them dozing on the slope, hatbrims down, poles stuck low over the torpid stream, gunnysacks ready for a catch (of pike, not carp or bullhead) they may never bring in, and they've looked content with the place that seems to belong to the old. No one young or middleaged is attracted to it, nor was I today; I must have a spark in me yet. I nosed the truck into a weed-lot the fishermen's tires have devastated and switched off the engine. I'd walk on from there.

The public history of Lindgrens' is safe and simple to recount. A man brought the name to this side of the river in 1870 or so, and being among the Swedes who foreran the great Norwegian move into the Territory, he had a first choice of homestead and claimed an acreage next to the riverwoods so that his house would be protected and there'd be water handy as he dug a well. Pete Johannesson's dad was in that group, Anders Hedin's too. The Hedin farm adjoins the Lindgrens' on the south, and all up and down the Red there is a thin settlement of Swedes who may live in North Dakota but go to Nora to trade and pray. Their living sites, tree-secluded and backed by gulleys and the river, charm the eye in a way the usual prairie farmstead cannot; it is attracted to these covert residues of Swedish woodland tradition. Pär Lindgren built across the neck of a huge eastward-looping horseshoe bend, its thirty acres all forest until he began cutting and clearing to make pasturage. He didn't remove the whole woods, just the outer half, and even there he spared some black oaks which still dot the prevailing meadow behind the stead. I've heard that in old times his and Johannesson's were the showplaces of the county: discreet haciendas painted white and grey with red trim, the lawns trimmed by flowers. He and his wife had many children but I don't, and don't have to, know the names. It is because the farm has been unlived on since 1908 that the public history of Lindgrens' is so attenuated. Some say that Pär wanted to escape his neighbor Lars Hedin, a misanthrope who seeing the devil in everything became demonic himself, but the truth of it has been of no importance to the living township; when people leave, what they said and did and why and who they were depart along with them, and only the one name marks the abandoned spot like an epitaph. To me, the Johannessons have always owned and tilled the land Pär broke, their skewbald cattle grazing in his meadow and his yard too, barbed-wire fence discouraging entry, and the mad Hedins have always been present to the south, blocking the way and thus completing the farm's isolation. I've had no telephone business that side of the Nora bridge, so I can safely end my account here. The rest—the Lindgrens' dreams and fears, the later illicit hunting or skating parties, the young romantic rendezvous—belong to a private history I wasn't conscious of today as I took my straw hat and set myself for a green retreat.

But the private account was beginning, and I tried to suppress it through indecision: should I bring the rifle? A clean, oiled .22 single-shot rides with me in the cab. I seldom take it out, target shooting doesn't please me anymore, and I've never liked to kill game. I do carry it, unthinkingly, when I go deep in the woods— an event rarer than the woods in Hedmark Township. This afternoon was such a time at last and I wanted to reach for it, but the urge seemed wrong. Perhaps I was reacting, like Art, who had carefully avoided mentioning the Rosenbergs, to the spell of last night's murder and was afraid the gun would somehow link me to it. Pulling the .22 from its sheath and holding the smooth stock in my hand, routine moves, were enough to end the wavering; but as I started along the drive, I was aware of the gun's full weight.

Wren summer, the tenth of May to August tenth, is the marrow of the season and was long passed now. Those quick midget birds have time for only the best of the north and don't stay to see the greens turn ripe and tire or the gold brilliance of stubble overtaking the prairie,

strewing its light like dust onto the outposts of wild vegetation. But I'm at home in early September, when the hues of grass and weed and tree-leaf begin to intensify towards bursting and the sky cools so that I don't have to squint into it; the soft, shortening days before autumn are a kaleidoscope in which I review the spectacle of the life of every being and thing on earth. This is their visible merging moment. As I perceive the outlines of the whole they make, I am comforted and do not fear the end. But if I'm preoccupied with humans and trapped in the small mechanic world they've set aside, I don't look for repose in nature. Then I love its violence, its acts of destruction and birth—tornado, thunderstorm, blizzard, avalanche, quake—and I become an ally in its war on man, who should feel awe at the planet's *élan vital* yet always needs to be reminded. The wars of humanity do it too, providing the storms in a limited world. I don't think they teach respect for nature; one comes back ready to sentimentalize it as apart from the death-drama and only gentle and green. I may not be so illusioned. I've watched battles in what seemed to be a quiet pasture and known that they weren't minor to the ants. The great pulse is incessant everywhere, and even today I could sense it beneath the skin of the landscape and my own. Strolling south above the warm, noiseless river and finally entering the mosquito-song of the woods, I was still inattentive to the meaning of the place that lay ahead; I just ported the .22 and whistled *It's a Long Way to Kholmogory*, a tune that recalled the bitter high spirits of some young men who were lost in a strange country and hoped to get at least that far home. I wondered if it had been the experience in north Russia that turned me to nature. Those forests were not all dread. People taught me mistrust of my kind, Whites and Bolos and peasants and doughboys and tommies and poilus and the soul-spent folk of Arkhangelsk, not the woods my comrades bled in which held a little danger but no treachery. The yen I developed was for solitude and to seek it I had, of course, to get away. What I've done is more than a withdrawing, though; some things, peace among them, are to be *found* in my so-called retreats. The city loneliness I might have had would have been vacant—nothing to *go to* in a space robbed from the human world—while here I could perpetually rediscover myself in the details of the whole.

There was a movement. I stopped. The Lindgren drive was now just a tunnel through dark greenery, straight at this point. The sun lighted a wide patch about thirty yards from me, and in it I saw a barbed-wire gate beyond which the way curved left and down and vanished. That would be the entrance to the farmyard. The branch in the clearing was still in motion, and I knew from the range of its wagging that whatever had sprung it must have been heavy. A logcock would have cried in flight; there had been no sound. Perhaps it was a hawk on the hunt or an owl napping. The branch was too high to have been jostled by a deer. Mine were not the calm deductions of a naturalist and I wasn't thinking like a game-stalker; I felt scared as a rabbit. The impulse was to fall prone and try to get that sniping Bolo before he could open up, then wait and be silent in case there were more, roll to the bushes, let them walk past, shoot—but I only put a cartridge in the gun, the mosquitos helping me, my heart at work. This had never happened. On previous walks I might have been startled a time or two by things *I* had startled. Such incidents are part of the country's delight. It wasn't until this afternoon that the sense of danger secreted in my thoughts and dreams of Russia became unmistakable experience. I could reason it off: no matter what had moved, there was nothing in this place at this hour to be afraid of. But I knew I could not continue. The wire gate and the sinistral bend marked the edge of a territory that now seemed prohibited, and I couldn't go where I didn't belong. I stood unbreathing a while, watching through the gun-sight as the sweat and the mosquitos collected, and when an oriole flew to the branch I gave up. I'd take some other path. How did I excuse it to myself? Perhaps Johannesson was over there to check on his cattle and I was recoiling from a sound I didn't know I'd noticed. Perhaps I'd simply lost the exploring mood. I worded none of this, nor did I think of the *Lindgren* name; my head was full of the war. I just backtracked to the start of the woods and poked a trail down the bank to the Red, where I could sit safe and invisible. Russia was not like North Dakota. There the peasants stayed in and around the villages, and but for the war one could have tramped the forests without being seen. As it was, any hint of human presence meant trouble.

For many years I tried to write my story of the campaign. People seemed so ignorant of that sequel to the Great War, so apathetic, that I wanted to give them a dose of it. Language wouldn't cooperate, however; I didn't have the right words, only the newsmen's rhetoric I'd heard both leaving and returning, Western Front verbiage that may have thrilled but did not inform. If I myself had had an understanding of the truth, language would have been there, but the confusion of

those last days and the shipping out of Arkhangelsk and the arrival here remained through the '20's, '30's, and '40's and kept me dumb on the subject. A story must be *known* to be told, and the writing follows. When I sailed away to the stirring academic phrases of our president, the truth was clear. I was no missionary, but I knew and approved the fight I was going to. My simple single-mindedness persisted at Stoney Castle camp in England, when Pershing ordered the 339th to Russia; the Kaiser had to be met on the west and the east, so why not on the north? I was almost glad to miss France (and England was so damned hot that summer). It persisted in the chill rain at the Bakaritza docks, though one hundred of the men aboard the *Tydeus* and the *Nagoya* and the *Somali* had died of influenza en route, and at beautiful Shenkhurst on the Vaga, nearing the farthest south our river gunboat crusade would take us. The promised *Huns* and *Finnish Whites* did not appear, but there was always some enemy, and it must have been late in the winter that he got one name and I began losing my sense of direction. In these long decades of wondering what happened and how, I've often gone for reassurance to a letter the regiment sent copies of to all the veterans of my outfit.

The Signal Platoon of the 339th Infantry, under Second Lieutenant Anselmi, has performed most excellent work on this front. Besides forming the Signals of the Railway Detachment, the platoon provided much needed reinforcements for other Allied Signal Units, and the readiness with which they have co-operated with the remainder of Allied Signal Service has been of the greatest service throughout. Please convey to all ranks of the platoon my appreciation of the services they have rendered.

E. IRONSIDE, *Major-General*
Commander-in-Chief, Allied Forces, Arkhangelsk, Russia
G.H.Q., 23rd May, 1919.

Perhaps I've most needed to be reassured that it did happen; there's been time to surmise the *why*. The letter, filed next to the discharge certificate of *William K. Sandness, #3455305, Corporal*, has been like a ratification of my hermit career, its very existence a charm against the truthwarpings of news and Helmer Nelson. While no one, not even he with his Columbia Encyclopedia, thought to accuse me of lying, people instinctively rejected my experience since it did not fit into the cartoon of history. The Great War's end is a railway coach in France;

the caption, *November 11, 1918*. Any chance for a picture of doughboys on the Dvina was wiped out by the second war, when representations of *convoy* and *U-boat* and *Murmansk* preempted the north Russian tableau. I used to talk about the war to Art in the old days, but in the clangor of the '30's I had gone mute. *The American forces did not participate in the fighting between the Allies and the Bolsheviks*, and what could one who had been there say? Then the parodists created a new ally, Uncle Joe. I became unbelievable. It was not that I attempted to speak and so suffered, just that to the sedative Hedmark way of thinking Helmer was easier to take. Some of them too had supported the Hitler-Stalin pact, and if his rejection of Nazism (after *June 22, 1941*) was more abrupt than theirs, he was a notable *character* and they understood the skit. My rehabilitation coincided with the eclipse of Helmer and Henry Wallace. When the Berlin air-lift and Hiss and Korea and McCarthy and the Rosenbergs invaded the screen, the silence around me began to diminish; people aren't shy of looking at me now. There's also been a clearing inside. I have not had to reread the general's reassuring note since the day another general became our president, saying *we shall never try to placate an aggressor by the false and wicked bargain of trading honor for security; Americans, indeed all free men, remember that in the final choice—a soldier's pack is not so heavy a burden as a prisoner's chains*. It is a nicer cartoon. Both young #3455305 and the old Villy Sadness are in it, and now there's no more mild shame in remembering.

I sat in my shady perch a couple of feet above the murmuring olive surface of the Red and let my eyes ponder the sunlit trees on the opposite bank. It was thirty-five years ago this month that we moved up the Dvina and the Vaga, and somehow that first campaign sticks intact in my memory while the rest survives as a mishmash of detail. Because we were new to the place and the action, events seemed to cohere; there was a perceptible line and hence a story. We had left sickness and the sea and Arkhangelsk behind, also a dispiriting mood that had nearly infected us. If I were to pick one word for the state of the north Russian people when I met them, I'd say *tired*. Arkhangelsk was large but now it was packed with refugees and foreigners, its streets a motley of man. Allied troops were everywhere, misplaced diplomats as well, and the conniving, incompetent British had taken charge. I don't know what I was expecting of the Russian faces that awaited us in the drizzle; smiles, perhaps. We *had* come to liberate them. But they hardly looked at us or they saw through us and beyond, and in no case did they stop to talk—benumbed figures in soiled, dark clothes and always lugging something, a bag, a valise, a bundle, and plodding onward. When they weren't impassive they were hostile, especially the seamen, who, an officer informed us, were *diehard Bolsheviki* and the cause of the shooting we heard at night; but they too seemed weary as they glowered from the decks. I escaped the lassitude of Arkhangelsk before it could get me. 1st Battalion was to push south on the Dvina, and Captain Odjard and Lieutenant Mead of Company A needed two field telephone specialists; so I and Private Bud Stokolwitz were detached from the Signal platoon and sent out with the slow tug and barge flotilla that would unplug the river all the way to Kotlas, where a legion of Czechs, now fighting in central Russia, was supposed to make contact. There were a lot of Signal men on the water, two per company, but we knew no more than the honest doughboys did. *The Bolsheviks*, hearsay went, *have accepted German alliance*, and the 1st would have to be prepared to meet the Hun himself—or his White Finnish comrade. We started our chug upstream, the clouds at last blowing off, the sky and sea pale blue, the land deep green and grey, not worrying much about the designs of General Poole; this was the war we'd been reading of, and the enemy, and once free of tired Arkhangelsk we could joke and loose our enthusiasm. The country we passed into was all forested lowland. Being from North Dakota, I couldn't have named the evergreens that the immense width of the river kept so distant by day. But the sight and smell of wood dominated our journey. We'd camp under a natural roof and sleep in the trees' perfume, and their height would gird our morning course as we breathed the wood-smoke of the tugs and continued up the never narrowing Dvina. The few shore villages made no trouble. Poole's Scots and Serbs had already taken these reaches en route to Bereznik, where we'd have a *job to do*, the Captain promised. Thus we enjoyed a hundred fifty miles' illusion, eating and talking and sightseeing like boy scouts on a trip, and if we saw a peasant, we'd wave. An occasional returning boat would offer monitions: there'd be wounded aboard. We were not permitted to slacken utterly. But when the shooting began—an antique tug, identical to ours, met us firing at the Vaga—I thought there had been some accident or mistake. It had been a placid, bird-watching afternoon, and this uproar of guns and voices did not follow. Perhaps there were juveniles in the tug and it was a game. *Down, dammit!* the Lieutenant shouted. We had stopped between the tug and an Allied barge that happened to be carrying artillery, and the Bolos were so close that the shells had to be aimed right over our deck. It lasted no longer than a football play, the tug hit and retreating, one of ours in pursuit, and we were standing again and smiling in wonder at what he had learned of the forest's inhabitants. The next two battles were also skirmishlike. I stayed waterborne with Company A, which did not take part in the land action that secured Bereznik but was assigned to open a front on the Vaga; and we transferred to the old holiday paddleboat *Tolstoy*, a souvenir of romantic peacetime. The sun and the scene and the boat combined to restore our vacation mood. The enemy didn't try to spoil it. Vaga was a grand river, clean and strong with high banks, and I counted more eagles than Russians until the bulbous silhouette of Shenkhurst appeared. It sat on a bluff. Many people had climbed down to greet the *Tolstoy*; finally, we got the kind of welcome the news had led us to expect. I'd seen peasants in Russia, but here were the merchants and whiskered holy men of a large spa town that was both rich and religious, and no one seemed sad to be rid of the Bolos, a handful of whom had been waiting unwanted in the square up to the day of our arrival. This place had all it needed—I think of the heaping tables, the well-dressed women—and so embraced the Company as its protector against change. Shenkhurst enchanted me. I have often wished I'd come to it in a different time and had a year to learn those tilting streets and the insides of those domed churches, perhaps to fall in love; I even wished it then. But the two glimpses I had, first on the advance, last on my early retreat, were enough to give materiality to the meaning of the war. Captain Odjard left a headquarters detachment at Shenkhurst, and I, specialist that I was, had to go on with him and Lieutenant Mead and the boys to take the farther south towns of Rovdino, Ust Padenga and Puya. The action was iterative: we'd approach, the Bolos would flee, and the peasants, their smiles not so avid as the merchants' had been, would let us occupy; then the Bolos would shell, we'd evacuate, and the peasants, bringing their trunks and aunts and cattle and samovars, would follow us by cart. When we regained the village, they'd go home and unload. If we did not, the peasants would fall back with us and camp in the next town, watching as we unmoored the *Tolstoy* and plowed away to bombard their huts from the river. We lacked the men to garrison every point; I reeled a lot of wire that early autumn. I also tasted the panic of sniping warfare. The Bolos fought like partisans in the thick, wet woods, but they weren't many either, and as long as the ground was soft, they'd attempt no *major offensive*. We did manage to establish a kind of front at Nijni Gora and Ust Padenga. The peasants who'd withdrawn to there would have to dig in and stay – unless they chose to join their revolutionary compatriots, and only a few single men went over. Most of them seemed not to hate us. We were strange, but the fear we evoked was nothing to what the Bolos aroused in them. I remember the harvest festival near Ust Padenga, a session of dancing and singing and drinking homemade *braga* and monstrous eating, to which the *starosta* or village patriarch had invited us along with the refugees of Rovdino and Puya, and how I was caught up in the warmth of an ageless earth-bound tradition until I forgot I was wearing a uniform. If we'd come to invade, so had the Bolos; but it was the men of Company A who were handed pies of salt fish and cabbage. As the nights lengthened, the Vaga began to recede. I was in a group ordered to Shenkhurst and rode the *Tolstoy* on its last Allied cruise. Thanks to my promotion, it was not I but Bud Stokolwitz left to *stabilize and hold* the winter front – and to die in the January massacre at Nijni Gora. I arrived a corporal in the town I'd been thinking of, my luck due more to what I *hadn't* done, not balking, not running, than to excellence in combat, and spent both of my two short days' reprieve in search of churches and women. That interlude ended with giant snowflakes, ice at the Vaga's edge. *November 11, 1918* was insignificant in Shenkhurst; even when we heard the news of armistice it did not apply. But I recall the day because it found me there and because of an incident I observed. I had strolled to the peasant outskirts of the city. I might not have done so alone in Ust Padenga, but the forests around Shenkhurst were said to be safe. I descended the hill and was about to turn onto a street that followed the riverbank south to the beginning of the woods, and at the corner, just as voices grew audible, I saw a long dark row of people walking. A bearded man in vestments led them chanting, and in their midst swayed a new pine box. No one noticed me join the procession or cared. They looked immured in grief, some wearing exaggerated sightless masks of it and howling intermittently, some calm but rolling their eyes to the opaque heavens, out of which white rags of snow were dropping, and the only guarded face was that of the corpse. He lay wrapped in a yellow robe on top of the shut coffin lid. At times a woman would brush the snow from his cheeks, but everywhere else it remained, lading the earth and the roofs and the branches and, to our right, the gelid Vaga. Yet he seemed terribly exposed; they all did. Mourning had rent the human husk and now their inner lives were open to the air. I was both touched and sad, as though I'd found a nest of kittens in a threshing machine, and harvest to start tomorrow; being so vulnerable, they couldn't know the risks of it. When they entered the forest I trailed along in hopes of attending a Russian burial. The graveyard would be near, else they'd have used a cart. I was not ready for the shooting. There was a quick burst and the procession stopped and became a swarm. I dove out of their way and took to the underbrush, my hands seeking the gun I didn't have. The priest stood alone by the upset coffin and scanned the trees ahead; his censer was moving. The corpse, freed of the yellow robe, was like a dormant drunk in the middle of the street, and the woman crouched next to him, still brushing off the snow. Another figure, a man's and in black, rested motionless a few yards behind, and another woman knelt there, groaning and hugging him. Their screams had sounded rehearsed, as if they'd been expecting the unwarranted blow. The shots and the flight were over now and a weary silence held the remnants of the procession. I knew some words in the language, but not the ones for warning *get down* or *go back*. The need of it was passed, however; instinct told me the sniper had left. I approached them with care to show I was unarmed and a friend, and only the priest took note of me, shrinking a bit until he recognized the uniform. The thurible twitched, its odor strange to the place. His headdress and beard were wet; his eyes, pale grey, and I couldn't read them. The man who had been shot was dead and his woman had ceased to struggle. The corpse's widow had sheltered him in the pall and sat there whispering. I didn't understand. Was it a private killing, or were the Bolos investing Shenkhurst? I could check for evidence, and I quickly found the tree where he'd hidden and the spent cartridges, saw the two sets of tracks he had made, the one wider spaced, but that was all I could do; nothing identified him or his point of origin (though he hadn't come straight from the city) or disclosed what he had meant. There was a death and there were vanishing footprints. The news had soon reached Colonel Corbley. As I got back to the scene the first Yanks were double-timing up and a number of male mourners returning in their wake, and the priest was trying to move the bodies and the women to the roadside.

Our search got nowhere, of course; snow obliterated the quarry's path. *November 11, 1918* sank into premature evening, a day of celebration in the west that in north Russia marked the start of the Bolos' *winter offensive* and the loss of the Vaga front. We had good officers and men but we were outmuscled, and Poole's replacement General Ironside chose to quit the southern salient. Each month we became more confused. Ironside was a master of tactics and strategy, and we admired him; it was just that those above him seemed lacking in purposefulness. The news from home didn't help. Stories of the Paris Conference filled the papers. No one wanted to read about us, and when journalists could not avoid mentioning our campaign, they'd give it a sullen inch. Ben's letters were representative in that they'd begin, *Say, haven't they told you the war is over.* The enemy also worked on our minds. He made sure that we'd read *The Call*, an English-language sheet printed in Moscow. Bundles would be air-dropped, or left in a village we were set to take, and there was never a shortage of copies in the big towns. *To the Allied Troops: Your Russian comrades greet you. We are men of your own class and know the hardships you have suffered in pursuing this interventionist war which the arms magnates and profiteers of the West have forced upon the Russian people. As friends, we must warn you that the cause you have been made to serve is doomed. Revolution is stirring in all lands, and the workers of the world are poised to bring the bosses to their knees and seize the means of production. Refuse to fight before it is too late! Lay down your arms—or turn them against those who would unjustly drive you into more needless slaughter!* The Wobblies had already treated us to such rhetoric, and the fellows I talked to shared my distaste (and I wonder how *they* got through Helmer's millenium); but in spite of our integrity, the wooden crosses were accumulating. I missed the shelling and the abandonment of Shenkhurst, for I was reassigned to the old platoon in Arkhangelsk where I waited out the rest of the war as Lieutenant Anselmi's lad, though I did train less-experienced men in how to string wire in battle, was along on the Pinega sortie, and used the telegraph at Allied Headquarters; yet I could not forget the town of church domes over the Vaga and its women and the day I partook in a funeral drama that time was making stranger and more meaningful. Ironside was instructed to *hold*, not advance, to substitute White Russian units for ours, and as the spring lolled on my confusion became angry. I knew the Whites would lose.

There were tough, skilled soldiers among them, but they had no pride of outfit, no cohesiveness, and the ranks seemed so damned tired. If a man showed spirit, he'd soon go to join the Bolos. The publishers of *The Call* must have had a talk with the Allied High Command: they didn't advance either, leaving us unmolested in our fortified delta. But everything beyond their lines was lost, Yemtsa, Rakula, Shenkhurst, every village and patch of woods we had fought over, and it wasn't much of a *way to Kholmogory* now. In 1919 we were ignorant of the communists' social program; still, I had an inkling of evil. The pious, inveterate north Russians were in for the change we'd come to avert, and there would be more and more wailing processions and gunfire and tracks in the snow, and what angered me most was the thought of their helplessness. Had Wilson and company allowed it, had they reinforced us, we might have given all of Russia to its people; but the noble Western democrats were exhausted too, and God knows if today the women of Shenkhurst are smiling. In my young altruism, I wanted to stay and continue the war like a Robin Hood, hiding in the forest, sneaking truth to the people, protecting them, and when the ship sailed, I was sick to the heart. Our crusade may well have been wrong, I said to myself, but we trebled the wrong in forsaking it. Youth rebounds, however, and as gulls squired the ship into the cold crystal beauty of Beloye More, a sea no longer white in the June sun, we began looking at each other and seeing *gallant doughboys* in triumph, not beaten, just stalemated in one part of a won war, and we went laughing home to share the victory. Doubts and bad dreams had years in which to brew—while two hundred forty-four Yanks, under wooden crosses, were becoming north Russia and the footprints multiplied.

We had an ancient sun-worshipper's view of death. *Going west*, we called it. Perhaps in our minds we were sailing to join Bud Stokolwitz and the others who had taken the short route. I know that I was impatient for America, to be in Elysium where I belonged, and I planned to get my discharge and travel the whole wide country. I hadn't been friends with Bud, yet a mental snapshot of his round grinning face survived as a reminder of all I hadn't seen: his own Detroit; Slavic America; Jewish America; the South, New Mexico, the Pacific. It was time to learn the land. Cut loose, I bore straight on Hedmark—naturally, I should visit home before the trip, unload my gear and thoughts—but when I arrived and heard of the folks' death, my wanderlust died as well. Its instant melting showed up the insubstantiality of the dream. I must have used it to hide what *was* material, my confusion, though in 1919 I had other words to justify the change. Ben was alone and needed help, and the pay I'd saved wouldn't last me far, and I was a bit bronchitic and winded and nothing'd be lost in waiting a month or two; and then there were allurements I didn't phrase, like the beauty of the earth in summer and the vivid sky and a steeple midmost in the horizon. So my vast impatient energies grounded here. I tried traveling once, to Lake of the Woods and Rainy River, and it wasn't because of the Russian look of north Minnesota that I chose not to repeat it. No, I enjoyed the place. The forests around Shenkhurst, or Baudette, had nothing to do with the evil men did in them. It was because of happiness my traveling ended in 1921. I wanted to choke the memory and I succeeded; to now, even the thought of travel has made me desperate. Better to stay in an understood farmscape, drive to Fargo twice a year, than risk new loss and the road. Safer to be *gone west*.

I am a cripple. I lie here awake at midnight, the house silent and dark around me, and feel the sting in my postwar wound. Living with it these many years, I became insensitive to the hurt; besides, it didn't inhibit the narrow routine I allotted myself. Tonight I acknowledge the wound and its depth. I have never been so uneasy, yet I dare to hope that this is the last twinge of healing. The uneasiness was latent in my afternoon watch by the river, thus I smoked a cheroot and sought comfort in the abstract cerebrations of a man. The war in north Russia was right, I decided, muddling but just. We went to restore to the people the governing of their own sweet, sad lives, wanting for them the thing we enjoyed: such tedium as is the blessing of Hedmark, where life is merely led. It wasn't they who opposed us but certain slaves of a dream which would uproot all that's natural, and since their warring began at the end of the West's, the dreamers prevailed. What started then was to continue along the Baltic and in east Europe and Asia and go on still. I was ashamed that we failed to protect those innocents but not that we tried; had I been young, I would have served in Korea. The threat seemed more terrible with each decade, the ignorance of the threatened worsening it—not just people, the inarticulate earth as well, for it was a threat to wholeness, to God. Times like these left no one a non-combatant and demanded that one act and speak truly (or be an *anti-Soviet*). I puffed at my cheroot and chuckled. Was I in fact deserving of Bob Rustad's admiration? Perhaps *I* should have been in his cell; the rhetorics were alike. But I wouldn't have killed. I realize, as he surely does not, that there's a bit of Helmer's poison dream in each of us.

The day was settling into its final quarter and my stretch of the river lay in shadow. A gaudy wood duck appeared swimming on the other side, its man-shyness forgotten. I had to go and eat and spell Ben at the switchboard, but of course I hated to leave. The duck was a sign of nature's opening, promise of a show that only a resting man may attend, and it seemed wrong to walk out; I shouldn't be so ready to allow the humdrum world its claim. Rehearsing the war, too, had secured me in the place. Such thoughts make one relish the present quiet. One grows addicted to war films and novels—to say nothing of news, provided it tells of elsewhere. (The news that Helmer Nelson has been shot is more upsetting than it should be.) But I stood and dusted my pants and soon was clambering with the .22 to the top of the bank. I was a man; my job, to scare the bird and skedaddle. When I reached the drive, I might have looked south to what I'd yet to explore, or even turned to brave it. The farmstead was close and I had the minutes it would have taken. I spared not a glance, however, just marched in the opposite direction as though leaving my uneasiness at the site. *Not today*, I said. Talking reinstated me in the world of live people; I could return to that of the Lindgrens tomorrow. The thing I'd come in search of would have to be waiting for me *there* because it existed only *there*, not in my head. Why was I hurrying? A car sat next to the truck, O. H.'s '39 Ford, and then I heard another live voice:

Pär Lindgren have a phone at last, Villy?

The late-fishing old boy had risen to piss and wasn't interrupted. He stared up at me, cackling.

Oh, I was over to hunt squirrels, I shouted, but shouting did not help the pain of the lie. I wanted to be in Russia. I was incapable of speaking truth.

O. H.'s sack lay folded on the ground. *So you had no luck either*, he said.

Not today.

Vell ve can try tomorrow!

I was glad it had been O. H., truth's walking symbol, who spotted me; anyone else would talk. He's also aware of my associations with that neck of the township—O. H.'s is the best memory around—but he is above gossiping. The fact would be stated, *Villy Sadness vas hunting down at the bridge*, and that's all. Others could speculate to the verge of untruth, not he. A moral historian watches; and until I did something to outrage him, like shoot a man or get shot, I'd be safe. (*It vas his own damn fault vhat happened!*) I drove the truck, a machine the age of his, onto the sun-reddened gravel of my old runway to Hedmark. There were more clangs in the engine than ever and the body seemed tipped a little to the right. I could afford a new one. The plants in Bud Stokolwitz's hometown have been working since 1946 and their products are the wonder of the country; I see a lot of sleek metal in the farmland. But I'll go on treating the known ills of the antique I have. A '53 dream would be no exchange. Next to O. H. I'm a kid, yet I too am a throwback to saurian times and hence unequipped for these. I too praise learning and esteem the traditional and uphold truth—except when I lie. My road to Hedmark was not smooth. I felt not self-propelled but towed into a west that didn't tempt me in spite of the hour's rich coloring, and the engine screamed and the body kept listing and dust gorged the air astern. Thinking can annul one's eyesight. I was blindfolded in thought, or non-thinking, and didn't wholly perceive the sun and the dust; I wasn't all of me in the truck cab. But the part that lingered knew that I'd have to stop and diagnose the trouble or I might not reach town. I did it, returned to my senses, in the lee of Odd Vinje's place. There'd be just a mile to go. The right front tire was down, hence the tilt. It was too low to drive on. I smiled, remembering how I'd lied about Nora, but not wholeheartedly: my handpump hose was ruptured. Now I'd have to borrow one from Odd, or, if the leak was too big, use his phone to call *central*. Ben likes to worry. Should I say another untruth to excuse my tardiness? It's not just the weaving of a *tangled web* that's salient, it's the *why*. I looked at the draining tire and wished I were in Kiev. An eastbound car arrived with the help I needed and the company I didn't; it was the new Engstrom DeSoto. Each evening, when the post office closes, Tina takes a bag of Minnesota mail across the Red and gets another, for North Dakota, in return. I don't know that she's paid, just that she'd be apt to do such a thing gratis. Tina helloed, a slim, good-looking woman of fifty-three in a '53 automobile, and stepped out to sympathize. If the black of her hair is inauthentic now, so what; the freckles are unchanged, as is Tina.

Are you all right, Villy?

No, I'm deflated. It was easier to joke than meet her eyes, and I kept mine on the problem.

You can borrow our jack to change it—yours isn't working, I spose.

I hadn't even thought of that, so insensible and Helmerish was I. *Well maybe I could try your pump instead. The one I've got is broken. I think it's a slow leak.*

Sure, I'll dig it out for you.

She went to open the trunk of the DeSoto, and I observed us as a stranger might have: two nice middleaged people who are mutually attracted but somehow bent on fighting it. This would explain my awkward tongue and her too sparkling benevolence. Tina and I know what it is, though; a vestige. Then she handed me the item that would save my day and asked about news, and I'd heard no more than she and Art and Ben and the rest—a man dead, a man in jail—and Tina said that Art was hoping to visit Bob and talk if the sheriff would permit, so maybe he'd learn something. I was going to use the pump and give it back to her, but she thought I might need it again on the road; I could drop it off later.

And where were you working this afternoon? she added.

A lie formed, but I caught myself. It was time to dismantle the web. I looked at her when I spoke: *Oh, I just took a walk by the river, down by the Lindgren woods.*

The stillness was huge and like a balm. Tina's eyes darkened momentarily; I could see the vestige in them. I could hear it in her voice too.

You haven't been out there for a while.

Must be thirty-two years. But I didn't go all the way in.

She turned to the east, as if hoping to find an answer in the horizon, and then to me. Tina's smile was deliberative. It's impossible to say a thing this long withheld.

Life is pretty good though, isn't it, Villy?

The last leg of the drive to town felt smoother. I pulled in at Harold Bakke's station and asked him to patch the tube and have it ready tomorrow. I could have fixed it myself; but I'm so well established as a repairman that my name can't be hurt, and Harold needs the business. I also wanted to test my guise. Had the turmoil been showing, I would have seen it on Harold. His grunt and his nod revealed no change. Only in saying a complete sentence, *they ought to hang that Bob*, did he depart from custom. I walked away. The town smelled of burnt meat. The supping Hedmarkers, were they to look out, would recognize one of themselves who must have stopped at

Harold's and think no more of it. Like him, they have a death busying their minds and *I Believe* to sing, and the sadness of Villy is less apparent than ever. I'd have to act to expose me; but if I couldn't do it then I won't now. Suicide is a limousine of a word, an aspiration to the soul-impoverished who by their act finally get a ride in it. Erik Rustad knew he was nothing. He used to denounce himself in the bar: *dis man ain't vert a shit, I tell you*. In jumping, he tried to become a someone—not a worse *character*, as he did. There were no Cadillacs waiting. The same would happen to me. People would decide that the act had been implicit in my name. But I won't do it, and it's because I've lost the urge I can speculate on those three syllables. They didn't mean much; I just wanted out of the then and there, to follow, and suicide was a permit. I chose the half-death of drinking at the start of Prohibition, so I might have gone it whole. I sat or lay drunk in my room, Ben waiting on me and silent, thank God, until Christmas when Tina came to the door with an apple pie and the drinking lapsed. There's been a bottle in my chiffonier. I didn't quit *in toto*. However, I've been plying that quart since the death of Stalin, and that was March, and it was a third full as I entered the house this evening and needed a drink. Ben had about finished his share of the meal—spuds and ham and beets, by the scent—and mine would be warm. He said nothing when I strode through the kitchen, and this was expected, but he didn't look up either; this was a reproach. I had business in my room to see to, steadying the soul, and the brandy was light as wine. I must have sucked an inch off that third. Sitting down to the table, I thought that *life* seemed *good*. The eats were.

What's the radio got to say, I asked him.

Oh, they're still talking about the big social security act that passed. The clock showed 6:30: I was late. But his nonchalance indicated that my punishment was over. *Ike, he's made some friends, I figure. That other thing was on the news too. It's gonna be an arraignment in Wahpeton.*

I suppose.

That was all's interesting. They sell you a tire today?

The web was apart now. *I didn't go to Nora like I thought. I took a walk over by Lindgrens'. Didn't make it to the farm though.*

Oh, there's where you went, he said, studying me with magnified eyes. They always appear incredulous; his world's a puzzle.

Maybe I should have bought a tire. The old one on the front was low. The truck is at Harold's.

Vic Vang called. His kid was burning dry branches and it got to a pole and the line. He wants us out in the morning.

Might have to string some new, hah? I'll check the damage and see. Then I'm going back to Lindgrens'. Haven't been to that place since 1921.

I guess it's a while, said Ben. My disregard of the text of the monologue was paining him; no milk or sugar in his coffee, but he kept stirring it. The switchboard sounded and he rushed out, though I was due on duty.

I didn't reach vertigo tonight, but I'm glad I'm no drunker than this. Once Ben had withdrawn to his own room and radio, I got a tumbler of brandy to help me into the shift. The years have taught me moderation if little else, and I knew I'd know the limit. There was also the tempering presence of the board. I haven't drunk on the job ordinarily, just read books; but this evening I was not enticed by *The Life of Woodrow Wilson*. That Professor Wilson had retired ill of *brain fag* in 1919 while Professor Bergson returned to his desk was unimportant. A shooting had closed the case — and it wasn't the war that needed analyzing. I took the brandy as a mnemonic stimulant.

First I rang the Engstroms to thank Tina again and say they'd have the pump in the morning, or so I told myself. She was home but Art answered and I felt a pinch of disappointment. Her voice would have been the second stimulus I wanted.

Then, raising the tumbler, I opened the public history of my life with Ingeborg, a too short unwritten book and as *safe and simple* to review as the tale of the Lindgren farm. I have done it before. Everyone in the township has. The ending makes the whole reducible to a sentence, and I've been a handy memento, thus no one's forgotten. Where others put the beginning, I don't know, but not I'm sure at *syttende Mai* 1918; who could have seen the scenes in the mind of that young traveler? People may start it with the homecoming, a Sunday the image of the one I'd left on (minus the bunting, of course), when I marched past in uniform as church was letting out and stopped to greet her though I'd not yet been to the house and been told. Yes, that's likely where they put it: at the late, unbecoming arrival of a man who seemed happy his parents were dead. *There* was the mark of the sadness to come. I was unaware of all but the shine of the day, and Ingeborg, whose touch completed the year's circle; and if I noticed something more than amusement in her green eyes, in her tone as well, it didn't affect me. I had earned commiseration.

So you're home at last, she said. *We were wondering.*

I had some mopping up to do in Russia, that's what prolonged it.

We hadn't written. I did send her a postcard from Arkhangelsk—another to Tina, just to stick to the rules; a postcard, like a hello in the street, presumes no intimacy. My grinning must have looked shameless. Tina stood next to her, but now the two weren't alone. Art Engstrom was at Tina's side and Jake and Selma Revland were at Ingeborg's. They all shook my hand, and the welcome seemed sincere if a bit reserved. Civilians who've been in church speak low, I thought. I was too used to the yawping of doughboys.

You have a load of work ahead of you, Mr. Sandness. Jake had immigrated in '98, the son of good middleclass Bergen folk, and was renowned for his elaborate old country grooming and manners. The township distrusted his genteel ways, his near perfect English; these didn't befit a man of the sod. Yet people could not get past the wall of courtesy he'd raised around him, so Jake was at least respected. Dad and I had serviced the Revland phone, and the place was attractive and Jake polite, but he had meant nothing to me until I awoke to his daughter. It was wondrous to be with him on the church lawn that day, to be dubbed *Mr.* in front of Ingeborg, and by someone she loved. The resemblance struck me—even her ash blond hair was Jake's.

You boys did such a fine job over there, said Selma, a plump brunette unlike her man and only child, *we don't know how to thank you.* She was a Swede, sister to Pete Johannesson, and spoke in a cradle rocking rhythm. I've heard mixed marriages were rare in 1900; no township-born norskie would have had her. Jake, the Bergen original, did as he wished in this and everything, and in Selma he got his perfect foil. He was rigid and at time arrogant; she, soft and hospitable and almost gushing. I remember the massive lunch she'd serve us workmen, Jake's reproving stare. If he hadn't kept her checked, some used to say, Selma would have turned Revlandsgaard into a year-round social. But I knew her no better than him and was surprised when she hugged me. *Oh, it would have been nice to have had things unchanged and waiting for you*, she said, too mournfully it seemed, *but God willed otherwise and I'm sure you'll try and make the best of it.*

I didn't see Ma and Pa and Ben in the crowd. Tina took me further aback. Was she starting to cry? *He should go home and rest now.*

If you need any help with the business, said Art, giving me a tap on the shoulder, *you let me know and I'll pitch in.*

I strove to read their looks, especially Ingeborg's; it was not quite so tragic. They thought I'd been told, of course, and perhaps was playing brave, but she had an eye on the *gallant doughboy* and not just the orphan. The bewilderment I'd hoped to leave in Russia was catching up. Something felt wrong. I gave Ingeborg the wreck of my smile and waved to the others and took my duffle and ran through the quiet, unpaved streets of Hedmark, elm boughs dozing overhead, to the place I should have gone right away. Ben was sitting at the board, innocent and responsible, and the shades were already pulled. He didn't speak of *them*, only *it*: *it* had happened three weeks ago (when I was still on board—the wires he'd sent were also to catch up). *You and I will keep the business going*, he said.

The thought of that little pratfall at the church would heat my ears, at least in the first month. But sorrow expunged the embarrassment, as, by the same process, rallying to Ben expunged my sorrow. The folks had loved and liked each other both, and the Sandness household had been nice to grow up in; I was imbued with its benign stolidity, which their mere physical absence could not shake. They had gone out of the world together, and this too eased my recovering. Not all married couples are so fortunate. Thus losing Dad and Ma did not occasion a loss of spirit. On the contrary, I was all verve; and I think of the courtship period between September 1919 and May 1921 as the most brilliant time I've experienced. It mattered, of course, that few seemed to appreciate what I'd done in the war, but I had Art Engstrom to talk to, a girl to love, and youth to buoy me, and those months were like one long luminous spring.

The snow seasons went unheeded. I have to press to recall them. But it was in the first winter that I took to seeing Art at his folks' place. He and Tina were engaged to marry next June and she too would often be there. When they visited her parents I'd ride along, and Ingeborg would show up in the Boes' kitchen. The couple made a couple of us as well. Art never came to see me, though; and I was always inviting him or him and Tina. I had only to mention the post office and they'd look down. He got me alone one morning—I was helping him pitch hay—and told me the short dark tale of my brother's romance. They

Ben and were sorry and knew the sight of them would sting.

n't want to add to his troubles now, said Art in a voice the cattle wouldn't hear. I was amazed, also amused, that the old rhino had been roused to action. But I didn't express it, not to Art and not ever to him. It was hard, in such a bright, self-centered period, to live near someone else's ache and be unable to give comfort; I understood, however, and prattled no more at home about Tina's engagement or the Engstroms or the Boes or even, until I had to, Ingeborg and me. If I was to *be out*, I'd say as much and no more. Ben was wise enough not to ask.

When I sailed to Russia I didn't know much about *good music*, and a string orchestra concert in Arkhangelsk had been my initiation. The Whites had put it on to thank us. So I discovered that there was something in the world to listen to besides schottisches, marches and hymns. It was late in the winter of 1919-1920 that I saw an announcement in *The Fargo Express*. A company from the east would be performing *La Traviata* at the opera house Saturday afternoon. I decided to go and Art, who was also interested, thought we might make it an outing with the girls. The Engstroms had a good vehicle, and he would drive. Thus we were launched — Art and Tina and Ingeborg and I — as a foursome, and Ingeborg and I as two. But preparations were needed. Not only hadn't we yet been *out*, I had not even called at the Revlands' in the role of beau; and in those guardian days decorum was more than a word. Asking Ingeborg would be the least of it. She was to accompany Tina, and I my friend Art. I never *did* ask her, I think, so sure was everything between us. The onus lay on Ingeborg in getting her folks' permission, but somehow she managed it easily. Jake had seemed delighted that young people should want to hear *good music* for a change, she said, and what Jake moved, Selma seconded. Ingeborg emerged alone when we picked her up, elegant creature. All three of them were dressed to put me in my borrowed suit to shame, but with Ingeborg sitting close I didn't feel bad; it was the age of the rising hemline. At least one couple in that huge audience was ready for *La Traviata* — she had studied piano and knew of Verdi, and I was set to applaud before it began — and the opera bound us mutually to the life of high things. Art and Tina, who'd been singing *Margie* in the car, had to work to like it but were solemn and tried, confessing, as we supped at the Metropole, that the performance had been *quite an event*. The highways were dirt in 1920, and by grace of God there was little snow on them: Art had a flask of hooch. He sipped and sang, steering through the night, and Tina and I weren't demure. Ingeborg wouldn't touch anything stronger than the fruit wine Selma made, and I thought her judicious; but she let me hold her hand and I could have sat in the swaying darkness of the back seat all the way to Mexico. When I took her to the door, Selma opened it smiling, and I sensed approval. I was right. Later, I learned that Selma had written a short account of our Verdi pilgrimage and would have sent it to *The Richland News* had not Jake, man of mystery, intervened.

Always, in retrospect, our courtship has seemed inevitable. It did then too. The beginning stage, which ended with our trip to Fargo and winter, led naturally to the next, spring, and the gaddings of the foursome: church doings, picnics in Wahpeton and Abercrombie, movies, baseball games—I was pitching again, to show off. While we partook of no high culture, we couldn't be blamed. There was none of it to be sought. (Apologies to the late Reverend Tiseth, whose recital of a long Norwegian poem we attended; I didn't understand a hiss.) We went to barn dances, which did not improve our musical education but allowed us to touch in public, and I enjoyed these the more because Ben's accordion was temporarily silent. It would stay in its case until 1925. Helmer was also inactive. He'd quit his Sabbath leaflettings and become as much of a closed-mouth drudge as any hired hand in the township, and it must have been then he turned to the reading which was to change not his *faith* but his interpretation of the social gospel. We didn't think much about him—or about Ben, I'm ashamed to say. Art and Tina were at the close of a brief season of irresponsibility; their friends, in the midst of an immense one. The spring stage ended with the wedding, and of course I was best man and Ingeborg maid of honor. I knew Ben had received an invitation, but I was shocked to see him in the church. He even congratulated them afterwards, not a hint of ill will in his soft rumbling voice. I watched him stroll away. He wouldn't be coming to the party; besides, it was for the young, and his losses had aged him. I said to myself *poor saintly Ben*. A hot June wind shook the leaves. Tina didn't throw the bouquet to Ingeborg; she forced it upon her. We all laughed, but Ingeborg's eyes were serious. Now marriage had broken up the quartet and we wouldn't be able to play together anymore. Though we could visit Art and Tina, there was still no *us* they could visit and soon they might have a child; and only the law provided a means of restoring the foursome, or at least of simulating it. None of us had such words in mind. I think, however, we must have sensed the inevitability of what held us and which, in that ritual moment, had shown its magnitude. I felt sad and small behind my grin.

Their wedding left us on our own but under public scrutiny. Ingeborg and I had no doubts that I knew of; the township did. These were expressed in long glances and offhand remarks, yet anyone who'd grown up here would take the point. It seemed I'd have a few obstacles to overcome. There was my boyhood reputation, which my incredible tales of Russia had not helped. I might be good for a joke or a tall story, but marriage? The act at the church had sealed my name, and it was unpromising. Had the folks been well-to-do, people would have tolerated my idiosyncracy, let me *chase that nice Revland girl* all I wanted, and wagged their heads at the antics of someone who had the world in store, but as it was, even my two conceded virtues — mechanical skill and book reading — were not enough to expiate my lack of means. The business had just supported the four of us, and Dad had meant Ben and me to get outside employment in time; now we could *keep the business going* and have money to live and that's it. If I married, I'd need another source, other premises too. Our little home would not accommodate a second life. I was sure, however, that Ben wouldn't object to the marriage itself; it'd keep me in the township. The one great uncertainty was Jake Revland. What I knew of him led me to hope that my reputation would not be the theme of the unavoidable interview. Local bias didn't affect him, but, since I was suing for his only child, he would have considered the prospects of *Mr. Sandness*. Ingeborg and I had become a genial duet by August, and it was then I asked her the question I'd have to put to him, and she nodded yes before I got it all said. We were walking in the yard at the Engstroms', where Art and Tina shared the big house with his folks. Harvest was under way, and we had been helping, I in the fields, Ingeborg in the kitchen. The Engstroms' was still our meeting place, though we had *been out* alone; strangely, I'd yet to cross the Revland threshhold. I took her hand and we left the yard and moved into the quiet of the trees. Both of us were damp and sore at the work day's end and could not have looked the romantic pair, but to us we made an idyll. I voiced my last worry, *what will your parents think*, and it seemed she had been expecting that as well. *Mama's fond of you, I know*, she said as we embraced. *I'll have her talk to Papa and see.*

It's hard to understand his way of thinking, he's so reserved. Papa is a true individual. If the words themselves were not reassuring, Ingeborg's tone was. Everything we want shall happen, it implied; and with her pressed against me in the heat of the woods, I did not doubt it. Thereafter, things went of their own inevitable accord. I was borne along like a token monarch, who, lacking mundane power, had just to agree to appear for the sake of ceremony. The interview itself was stagemanaged, but I accepted my passive role.

Jake was a natural actor and made the most of his lines. Selma met me at the door and escorted me into the livingroom where he sat with a cigar and an open book, and as he rose, hand extended, I saw he had not taken off his church suit. Ingeborg remained totally invisible, her mother conspicuously. Selma would dart in and out replenishing our coffee and doughnuts, her fervid pantomime expressing how much she wanted not to disturb the men. Once she gave me a pat on the wrist. Jake ignored her throughout, and I supposed I should follow his lead. It was a chaste room, books darkening the walls, the smooth furniture and piano seemingly untouched, and it awed me speechless. But perhaps I wouldn't have to talk: this was Jake's setting, Jake's moment.

So good of you to call, Mr. Sandness, he said, and I thought he sounded more British than American. In the old country, he had studied our language under a Brit; Ingeborg told me later. *Mrs. Revland said you might stop by, and I'm glad you could. We have such a slow life here.*

Ingeborg's coaching, *don't rush him*, had failed to salve my nerves. I was ready to get the question stated and over with. *Thank you, sir*, I began, taking the offered seat. *I came about some business that—*

Oh, you did? We always relax on Sundays. There's so much work and business the rest of the time. On Sundays I like to think and read a book and do not much of anything, and if we're lucky enough to have guests, it's even better. I was just looking at a poem I learned years ago. Are you familiar with Ibsen?

He had not allowed my near gaffe to spoil the mood, the amiability of which was instructive. I, being fresh to the Revland theatre, did not understand that I was in the polite first act of a long drama, and that Jake had to school me. His was the main part now; mine the supporting. I had but to watch and listen and imitate, to *be there*, and he would give the cues.

I've heard of him.

Then you'll remember the poem, or at least the heart of it, he said, closing the book and gazing into space.

> *Stort har jeg mistet*
> *og stort jeg fikk;*
> *best var det, kan hende,*
> *det gikk som det gikk.*

Do you recognize that one? It's just a trifle, really; all poems are. But the written word is my weakness.

I'm sorry. I wish I had studied the language.

No, I should apologize to you! Poems are worth nothing. Books are nothing. Look at all these. It was quite a job bringing them over, but I was young and thought I had to have them. A man is tough when it comes to his weaknesses. Stort har jeg mistet og stort jeg fikk. Much have I lost and much have I gained, eh? I had given up the homeland; I had kept these books. But if I were to sit here every day I might get lost in them and the important things would fall to ruin, and one should remember why one came to America. A good life isn't built with words. So please don't think this is more than a Sunday pastime. I hope you'll be indulgent, Mr. Sandness.

Everyone associated with the girl a man loves is in her nimbus. I had no trouble admiring Jake Revland; had he been an oaf, it wouldn't have mattered. As it was, I saw a spruce, handsome, erudite man—who also resembled Ingeborg—putting forth his best to charm me. The setting soon felt comfortable and I like quite the pampered princelet. I was the oaf then.

Jake avoided intimacy. *He's so reserved*, she'd said. However, he wasn't shy of talking; that first act went on through much of the afternoon. I learned of Norway's political and economic failings, America's better system, the scenic splendor of the fjordland, Dakota's hidden beauty (which had to be sought with a plow), and of his gratitude in being here. I can't in truth remember all he told. It was to be a continuing drama, and the revelations of its many scenes are intermixed. He did not, I believe, say a word of Ingeborg or his wife—or ask about the suitor. Just one question arose. He had been discussing the state church of Norway. It seemed that people were becoming loathe to attend services, and this he blamed on dull and overlong sermonizing. *In America they keep it short and sweet*, he said, an eyebrow arched. *You're not an atheist, by any chance?* I wasn't, although (I did not add) the Reverend Tiseth might make one of me yet. Jake nodded and resumed his oblique self-portraiture. What he finished and presented to me that day was the sketch of a well-bred, sensitive, educated and somehow hurt individual; he had the air of one who'd risen in spite of undisclosed sad circumstances. I feared that *my* question would distress him.

At last he stood up, and I thought I must have missed the cue and would have to go home a failure. *I'm giving the gentleman a tour of the place*, he called to Selma as he walked me out. *You might take a trip downstairs.* She didn't reply. It was an attractive farmstead, the house and the barn and the machine shed and the chicken coop all painted white and not a speck of rubbish to be seen, but I was not too observant. Jake would have showed it to any visitor. I'd been a flop, and he wanted to let me off kindly. I trailed him through the yard, hands in pockets, awaiting the sign of dismissal.

The house and the barn were here when I made the purchase. However, they did require some work. The original settlers didn't need the kind of shop we do today, of course, so I had to build one. I also put up the others, learning carpentry on the job and botching it. I enjoyed myself, though. Now I'm confident enough to try building a garage; that's the next plan. I might get rid of the cattle. The land is too rich to waste on pasturage. Oh, I'd keep milch cows, but just one or two to supply the household. I think I'll add to the chicken flock; the market is growing. I'll have a near vacant barn for them. You're looking at an average agrarian enterprise, nothing out of the ordinary, but it takes a lot of sweat to keep it going.

What could I say but *it's a very fine place*?

He smiled, as though at a humble jest—or jester—and studied his nails a minute. I took his silence as a prompting. The yard was ovenlike and thick with the scents of animal and straw. Perhaps Ingeborg was at the window. I had the center of the arena, and all eyes were enjoining me.

Dependable help is hard to get, he said before I could ask, *steady, dependable help. I'd like to acquire more land and am in a position to do so, but, as you see, I'm the only man here, and the existing work is almost more than I can handle. Mrs. Revland's people help when they can, and there are seasonal itinerants; however, this place needs someone to work all the time, at least from planting to harvest. Oh, I know why I can't find anybody; it's obvious. The young fellows in America have so many opportunities to advance themselves—they're not to be blamed. That must be it, don't you think?*

Jake paused again; he had turned sober. The gist was beginning to penetrate my love-rapt consciousness. But I was still thumbing the script. *Maybe you could talk to Helmer Nelson.*

He treated my remark as the drollery it wasn't, and had to laugh. *Wouldn't that be something! No, we need a man who isn't set in his ways and could live here and associate with the family — a man of your age. No, hermits and theologians are out!*

Well, I said, picturing poor lone Ben, *I suppose I could do it — if you're interested. I'm obligated to my brother, you know, but I could arrange to help him part-time during the months I'd be working here. I'm afraid I don't have much experience —*

It was the breathless culmination of the first act. Jake looked at me square, his mouth revealing the joy he was too courteous not to try to hide, then stretched out a hand. *May I assume we have a deal, Mr. Sandness?*

Well, yessir. As I accepted the shake, I felt that both Ingeborg and her mother were watching and I wanted to make sure the *deal* was thoroughly understood before I saw them. Jake was guiding me toward the house. Has the moment arrived, I thought, or has it already been? *May be a coincidence, Mr. Revland, but what I came to ask you —.*

He stopped me with another laugh. *It's Sunday! There'll be plenty of time to attend to the details; all winter, I expect. You say you have no experience? Then you're like a certain other young fellow who came straight out of Norway and hadn't touched a plow in his life. But I learned, and you will too. We'll get to that and the rest later. Let's enjoy this day while it lasts and go inside and formalize our agreement. Eh?*

The nature of the rite he was proposing didn't trouble me, nor did the meaning of *the rest*. Instinct said I had won, and the beaming faces of Ingeborg and Selma confirmed it. He went right to the kitchen table where two full wine glasses stood, picked them up, handed one to me and raised the other.

Jake's hurry was clear evidence of thirst. *Ah, here we are: to Mr. William Sandness and his long and genial association with the Revland farm! Skaal!*

Skaal. That much Norwegian I knew; I also knew to drain my glass. The cool plum wine was no effort.

How are you, Villy? said Ingeborg. Her pale hair was tied back and she wore an apron. The women had been cooking. I smiled and said fine. By now I had smiled my cheek muscles sore.

Selma apologized for the heat of the room—of the weather too, it seemed.

But why don't you stay to supper? We'd love to have you.

Let's try it again, said Jake. However, the bottle was not in sight. He nosed around him like a detective, then stared in mock-reproof at Selma. *Mrs. Revland, are you going to have to take a second trip downstairs?*

Perhaps he wasn't funning. I could tell his annoyance, and Selma's; it was slight but enough to change the mood. *It's the end of this bottle,* she said. *I didn't have time to open another.*

Something prodded me to intervene: the clock, I'm sure. *Thank you for the invitation. I would like to stay, but I promised Ben I'd be there at six. It's my turn at the switchboard.*

Ingeborg's warm expression, unchanging, showed that she'd had no part in the tiff, but her parents were relieved. It was Jake who escorted me to Art's dad's car, which I had borrowed for the occasion—our service trucks have never been pretty. *Oh well, Mr. Sandness*, he said as he shook my hand goodbye, *best var det, kan hende, det gikk som det gikk.*

He didn't bother to translate those words, and I winked, pretending to understand them. I was naive to the point of smugness. It's embarrassing to think of how I thought at twenty. *The worst is over*, I told myself as I drove home. Yet my performance in that scene—the big interview, the first act, call it what I will—was to be evaluated and denounced. I didn't know that I would learn to hate Jake Revland and, because of him, the poet's lines: *Maybe it was for the best, things went as they did.*

During the final phase of our courtship, the engagement, I was given a chance to work out my weaknesses. I spent a lot of half days at Revlands', more in the barn than in the house with Ingeborg, and when the Hedmarkers saw me turn cowboy, they approved. Jake instructed me in the feeding and nursing and management of cattle—*the rest* he would get to in summer—and was most patient. He also stuck to the subject; there were no great monologues. Occasionally, I'd have to do the chores myself. Selma would stop me in the porch, whispering *Mr. Revland isn't feeling too good*, but, since I didn't need much guidance anyway, I'd be satisfied to man the cattle alone. Nor were there great toasts. The wine made but one appearance, on the Christmas table, and again the supply ran out; again I sensed conflict. That was the eve. Christmas Day, we were to go to Pete Johannesson's. The old man still survived there, but Selma's brother was married and running the place and he liked to have everyone celebrate the holiday at the ancestral home. But it seemed Jake had been *ill in the night*, so I had to drive the three of us to dinner. The Johannessons were told no more than I, and they expressed concern and forgot it. His illness was to be a presence in our courtship. Ingeborg did speak of it eventually: *I'm afraid the wine just doesn't agree with him. I get so worried about Papa—he must be allergic or something.* I'd smelled it on Jake, even seen a few bumps and cuts, but he had never acted the drunkard. To me, as to the whole neighborhood, Jake Revland was the model of moderation. Hearing the truth did not lower my regard for him. Dakota winters can be long and soul-straining and now, by law, they were dry; liquid medicaments were both expensive and a risk to use. I was young and parched and could not but envy the man who had all he wanted *downstairs*. Often, toiling, I'd think of Selma's plum wine and what I'd give to have another taste of it. She didn't offer it, though; externally, hers was a temperance household.

As the engagement ripened and our coming married life took shape, there were just two matters *I* had to attend to: Ben, and the rings. The fraternal talk went well. Ben agreed to my working part-time, May 1st to the end of August, also to guarantying a bank note so that I could visit the jeweller. We spoke of business, not love; had he disapproved the marriage, it would have showed in his mathematics. But the equation checked. I think he had been pondering it a while. When I told him that the wedding would be simultaneous with the start of the new schedule, he seemed happy. Ben has always disliked change. *And you'd be moving out then too*, he said. I would. Ingeborg and I were to live in the Revland house. It had been decided—how, I don't remember. Perhaps the decision made itself. Jake and Selma had a bedroom on the ground floor and Ingeborg's was on the second, and we'd be sharing the room in which she had grown up. I saw nothing wrong in this. I hadn't the money to seek an alternative. Besides, it was just for the beginning. There were other plans in genesis, plans having to do with an untenanted farmstead and Pete Johannesson and a home in the woods. I never got around to asking Jake's permission—no one reminded me—but I married Ingeborg in the May of that year. It was an elaborate wedding that filled the Hedmark church. Selma's people were not the only Swedes to come over from the Nora congregation. Reverend Tiseth spoke the words, in English, thank God, and his Mrs. sat at the pump organ, and Tina was matron of honor and Art best man, and Blanche Vinje sang *In the Garden of Tomorrow*, and Ingeborg was all in white, her cheeks pink behind the veil, and I doubt my own were pallid in the heyday of our life. Everybody adores a young groom; but I'd also earned public respect. I could sense it as we emerged in the May light, hear it in their gratulations. I'd become a son-in-law and an adopted orphan too, and the stigma was off. Yes, that was our heyday. Two months earlier, Warren Gamaliel Harding had been inaugurated President of the United States. He was a sorry individual, but his reign outlasted ours. There were photographs of the wedding. The Johannesons would have copies, Selma too. I burnt the ones we'd been given.

The switchboard was inactive this evening and the thrum of Ben's radio died early. I had ample quiet in which to nurse my thoughts and my drink. I'd set myself a conundrum: to tell what the township knew of me and Ingeborg, omitting what only I can know. It was an avoidance game, one of several I've played these years, and I didn't want to go on with it. There was such a divergence of public and private knowledge, especially in regard to our six months' married time, that telling less than both would be untrue. When we came back from our honeymoon trip and reported to Art and Tina and others, we didn't lie. Spring in the north woods *had* been magnificent, the lake huge and chilly, and we *did* have nice walks and a comfortable room, and those roads were as primitive as we said. The Sandness truck, which had seemed the right wilderness vehicle, did not have adequate springs. Jake's hundred-dollar wedding present had bought the gas and all. They could enjoy our true account and laugh with us and wish they'd been there, but what could they know? Women are supposed to sink to intimate gossiping among themselves; I doubt, however, that Ingeborg said a word to Tina of our nights in the Hotel Baudette. She was too sensitive — not so Tina when she was a bride. I talked with Art about many things, not that. Our happiness was like a shameful secret; we had to spare people. Perhaps, I thought, twirling the brandy, this is what I've been doing to myself. I was the one chosen and who chose to live, and mourning was the price of staying here. Mourning has spared me the bright recollections, kept me in hell and Hedmark, and excused me from getting over the loss and on. It's been a lot to pay. But it must have had some compensatory value, else I wouldn't be fighting the words that are coming now. Perhaps I have been waiting until I could tell them to Ingeborg.

I had to have another drink and continue. If it's sadness made Villy the man he is, *let's be it*, I decided. In the short hot season of 1921, the township and I were equally ignorant of what was to come; since we weren't able to look backward, we didn't think to look inside. I for one had little chance to brood. Working dominated the weekdays, Ingeborg and my parents-in-law the evenings and the Sabbath, and I was a zealous young sweaty machine with never a minute to myself — except when I sat in the shed Jake used to call *earth-closet* or *dass*. We dwelt in the Revland house and ate at the Revland table. While Jake and I were out with the team and the tractor and the cattle, the womenfolks took care of the chickens and the food and the cleaning and shopped in town. I helped Ben infrequently. He still had eyes to drive then and had hired old Mrs. Svensgaard to manage the switchboard when he got called. It was an animal summer; I had the spirits to match. But I was perceptive enough to notice something. Jake's illness must have remitted with the start of planting, for he was up every day and working like Hercules, a slight, taut, middleaged man whom even I could not outmoil. He'd added to his acreage and gained an unpaid hireling — though I was to receive a share of the crop and of the profits on the cattle — and he seemed gratified. When it was just the two of us alone he acted civilly; I remained *Mr. Sandness*. It was at supper, Ingeborg and Selma looking on, that his behavior became disturbing. He would cock his head and give an ironic half-smile and study me, or say apropos of nothing, *you're the son of the place now, what do you think*? His kidding tone would invite a harmless reply, but Selma would react as though he were stirring up an ancient antagonism. *Oh, let him eat*! she'd butt in, and Jake would shrug, his glance too cold to be conspiratorial. Ingeborg would be silent. Once, before we slept, I asked her if I had insulted Jake or wronged him in some way. *I guess he's been tired and a little sick*, she said quickly. *Mama's upset. He goes downstairs again, you know. I wish we could move this fall.* Jake's suppertime antics did not worsen until the end of harvest. The threshing crew had finished and I'd hauled the last load of wheat to Hedmark and Selma was in the midst of wine-making and canning and all of us were hot and grimy and bushed, and it was Saturday night.

There'd been a row of wagons at the elevator so I was a bit delayed and could not stop to watch the dimming of the land, the haze of threshing bringing sudden dusk; I just had time to run to the bath house and dream, as I scrubbed, of a giant steak and a hill of mashed potatoes.

The switchboard buzzed. Someone in the night needed operator; O. H.?

Hello, Villy, this is Jensine Iverson.

Yes, Mrs. Iverson. She was a rare caller. I haven't seen O. H.'s wife in Hedmark since the '30's, and it isn't often I hear her on the line. The clock read 10:22.

I was wondering, could you tell me if Ida's home yet?

I got up and raised the shade of the west window. In the moonlessness, I could barely see the squat brick building next door, once the township fire hall and now the home of Paal and Ida Malmlund and their two kids. There was no light, no car parked in front. The Malmlunds don't have a telephone.

It seems pretty quiet.

You suppose you could do something, Villy? Jensine sounded urgent. *I have to get a message to Ida, and it would be best to leave a note before they came, so you'd have to do it right away.*

Certainly.

Just say, if Ida and the kids want to sleep here with us, they're welcome. That's all. But I think you should hurry.

I wrote it on the pad and said it back to her. *Was there anything else I can do, Mrs. Iverson?*

No thanks, and I must thank you for your help.

O. H., the emblem of truth, raised his children poor. Ida's the eldest of five and in a respect the most unfortunate; she married a truant, childlike *character* with no more interest in moneymaking than O. H. ever had. Poverty drove all those kids out of Hedmark, soon as they were old enough. At the start of the second world war they dispersed to Fargo and Minneapolis and Seattle, Ida, I think, to the latter—she'd already married Paal and had a son—and most of them did and have done quite well. Ida didn't choose to be excepted; it's not she that people blame. Still, Ida's the only Iverson who returned, and in the same plight. I understand they had a shack on the Red south of Fargo where they spent the immediate postwar years and the daughter was born, but even so they were always around, Ida and the kids visiting Jensine, and Paal doing summer work at Jed Hoy's. Paal's machine shop job in the city would end when spring arrived; some thought he would quit in order to get back to the land. I don't know. I'm twenty years too old to have been friends with him and the Iverson kids and Bob Rustad, and all I'm sure of is that the Malmlunds looked luckless. They moved to town in 1948 or so, buying the fire hall—a hundred dollar transaction, according to gossip—and Ida signing on at the school district. She'd been a rural teacher in the late '30's, giving it up for marriage, and she was in the classroom now only because Paal could not support the family. He's still with Jed, of course; and last winter he did work at a gas station in Fargo. But their drab little home inspires much head shaking. These are boom times and anyone who isn't booming with them must be *no good—ya and it seems dey don't get along so vell on top of it*. The son, Peter, is a nice-spoken kid of ten or twelve whose unsmiling eyes record the strife they have witnessed. The girl isn't old enough to have the run of the streets, but he comes up to see us on occasion, and we give him a nickel. He's like an embryonic O. H. I pity him. Well, they're all about to experience a change of setting. Last May, Ida didn't sign a contract and let it be known that they were planning to try the west coast once more, Oregon, where Paal's folks moved in the '30's, and they've been packing and saying goodbye since the end of August. They're to take off tomorrow, I believe. While the locals doubt that Paal will *make something of himself out there*, I wish him and Ida the best. It's not to be had in Hedmark, not for them.

    I rolled the note and tucked it into the screendoor handle and went back to our stairs and crept up. The silence made me mindful of Ben's keen hearing, and each tiptoe sounded like the thud of a hammer. He didn't respond, though; I was able to reach the board without mischance. There were no irate yawns or coughs in the dark. Such a nonverbal coexistence as ours—the whole township's—requires attention to sign. Even our words are not what they denote: I had to listen between Jensine's. *You should hurry* meant there was something amiss tonight with Ida and Paal, and *your help* would be staying alert and, if necessary, callling. The name of the thing wrong was mine to imagine. In this I could draw on community intelligence, which knows of the Malmlunds' domestic trouble and of Paal's low standing among the Iversons as well; and it was no doubt at O. H.'s place, three miles from town, that Ida and Paal and the kids had been visiting. The boy spends a lot of the summers there, Ida and the girl too, so it followed that they would want to be with O. H. and Jensine on their next to last day in the valley. The decampment celebration, however it was, had gone on late. Perhaps some of Ida's siblings had arrived—the sons of O. H. love booze and not Paal—and there had been drinking, words, a struggle. Jensine had become so anxious that she'd rung me when the Malmlunds were driving out. But they still weren't here. The life of sign is also a life of patience. I could do no more for the moment than sit and sip brandy and think.

Selma had prepared quite a feast that long-ago evening; I could smell it before I got inside. She and Jake and Ingeborg were at the dining room table—usually we ate in the kitchen—and I knew they had been waiting. The women did not look up from their empty plates, but Jake rose to welcome me, his smile like a politico's. There were lidded bowls in the middle of the board, and I saw that Selma had taken out her finest cloth and oldest china and silver. She and Ingeborg were drinking coffee. Jake had a glass, an uncorked bottle next to it. The tension was as pungent as the food.

Glad you could come, Mr. Sandness. Here, let's give you an apertif—may I? It's a rare wine, the lady of the house is so jealous of it. We must enjoy it while we can.

I sat opposite Jake, and Selma faced Ingeborg, who had to hand me my glass. *I'm sorry I didn't get here on time*, I said to everyone. *There was a crowd at the elevator.*

Oh, let's dispense with the formality. We're not kings and queens, you know; we're just common people who work hard and live under one roof. I think we should have a toast to honor the completion of our first joint enterprise. Even the ladies will drink to that!

Ingeborg shook her head.

No, said Selma her mouth small and stern, *and for heavensakes—*

No, they say? No? Jake rolled his eyes in mock consternation. The bottle was half gone. *They spend weeks and weeks making it, and then they refuse to honor the son of the house? I guess you and I will have to perform the rite alone. Let's see, how did I phrase it? Ah yes: to Mr. William—.* He tabled his glass, which had been in skaaling position. *It seems I haven't taken my own words to heart. I was just saying we should drop the formal nonsense, and here I go! I hope you'll accept my apologies. Let me try it again: to William—or is it Willy, or Villy, or what?*

Well, I'm known as Villy.

I see; Villy. That's a strange thing to call oneself, isn't it?

I'd experienced malice in the army, but it wasn't like Jake's. This was elusive, elvish, planned. I didn't anger, though; months of brute physical work had evened my mood. *I suppose*, I said, *but I didn't pick it. Wish I could remember who did.*

Ah, you're saying that others call you Villy, but you don't. Am I correct?

Yes. But I have accepted the nickname.

May I ask how it is you call yourself then?

The chill of the wine glass in my palm allured me; if I stayed obliging, I thought, he'd have to get to the toast. Selma was the one who showed impatience. *Go ahead and eat now*, she said, uncovering the steamed vegetables.

Jake looked aghast. *Don't you see that we're about to skaal! One thing at a time, Mrs. Revland. I'm surprised at you.*

She backed down with a sniff of displeasure. I glanced at my bride, hoping for a clue as to what was expected, but Ingeborg seemed trying to shrink to invisibility. I was new in love, and it was love, much more than farmboyish complaisance or wine-thirst, that checked me then and until the last act.

All right, Willy—or Villy, or whatever it is—we may proceed.

You were asking the name I like to go by?

My, he remembered! Jake smirked, smug in the knowledge that I couldn't or wouldn't parry. The bout had just started so even if I *had* gotten mad he could have switched to the role of doting paternal tease and shammed amazement while readying his next thrust.

But I was game and smiled. *I think I do answer to the name Villy Sadness, even to myself. When signing, of course, I have to use the legal one.*

You have a legal name, too. Are we familiar with it?

Well, you must be. It's William K. Sandness. The K. stands for Karl, my father.

William K. Sandness—and you don't like to go by that name, your legal one, in the community where you live? He scowled. It was as though things had gotten out of hand due to the incompetence of a player (not Jake) and had to be stopped and studied. Perhaps my mentioning Dad had been a foul, or an admission of uncompetitiveness. When he spoke again, he resorted to the tone of an exasperated coach. *Young man, all we are attempting to do is to establish your identity—*

your name, in other words—so that we can toast your health. That's not too presumptuous, is it? I would have thought you'd be glad to cooperate. We're sitting here ready to drink and eat and the meal's getting cold. But no, you're unwilling to give us a simple answer. You're home among family—why be so evasive? All right, let me put it a different way. You have a brother, do you not?

Yes.

Does he have a name?

Ben, or Benjamin. I thought you knew.

Jake paused to concentrate on his wine glass, which he was slowly rotating. His voice became almost gentle: *Does he have a full name?*

Benjamin Franklin Sandness.

That is his full, legal name?

It is.

And your full, legal name is William—Karl—Sandness?

Yes.

Very good. Something in the glass amused him. He still sounded lenient. *Sahn-ness is an old Norwegian name. Sahn-ness. The d is dropped. But that's beside the point. Tell me, what do people call your brother?*

Ben Sandness, or just Ben.

Ah, and what does he call himself?

The same: Ben Sandness.

Not—Ben—Sadness?

I permitted myself a light laugh. *No, he's always had the names he was given. I'm the only—*

Sir, I want to pursue this. Jake would be kind but tolerate no mirth in the idiot or child he was addressing. *Let me review your position. You say that your full legal name is William—Karl—Sandness, and that you have a brother whose full legal name is Benjamin—Franklin—Sandness who's known to the community, and to himself, as Ben Sandness. You, on the other hand, are known as Villy Sadness, a nickname for which you claim no responsibility but which you have accepted. Now, the question is, why didn't they give your brother a nickname?*

I don't quite understand.

Nonsense! Jake's glass hit the table with his shout, and wine flowed at last—but on the cloth. *You understand perfectly! It was you who came up with the ridiculous nickname of Villy Sadness! You alone! If it had been other people's idea, they would have called Ben the same thing: Sadness! All we needed was a name to drink to! That's all you had to say! My! name! is! Villy! Sadness! We're sitting here and the ladies are starving to death while you—*

Present yellings interrupted those of memory. I hadn't heard them drive up, but the Malmlunds were home. Stepping to the window, I touched open an edge of the shade; I didn't want them to see me or my silhouette. Ida and Paal were indistinct, she standing next to the driver's side of the old Ford, he on the passenger's. The boy had a sack in his arms and was waiting by the house. Had the Malmlunds been conversing normally, they would have been inaudible. They weren't, and weren't.

You leave her where she is! Ida was mad, all right.

No kidda mine's gonna sleep in the car! It was hard to imagine Paal angry, soft-hearted slowpoke that he is—though he *can* irritate others; he must have been boozing. *I'm 'onna take and carry her inside and that's all there is to it!*

She's going to sleep inside at the folks', just like me and Pete! So you just let her rest!

Ya, I don't know how you plan to get there, cause I'm not driving you, sure's hell.

Ida paced around, fuming. *We're not moving to Oregon with you! We're not moving anyplace! You can go by yourself and live in a shack and take it easy, but the kids and me are staying here. And you think we'd drive with you? It took us a half hour to get home, you stopping and vomiting all the time! Good Lord!*

What's wrong is your goddam relatives interfering in my business! They have no right sticking notes in my door—and how the hell they managed that I'll never know!

Well, we can't stand out here like a bunch of raving idiots, said Ida, and marched toward the house. I had to strain to listen. *Pete, you take that inside. I'm packing some things and then Granpa'll come.*

She and the boy went in and Paal took the little girl out of the seat, handling her blanketed form with care. His legs were uncertain and he was talking low. Silence reoccupied the street

It sickened me, turned me sad to the stomach. I'm averse to the violent. I didn't leave Russia a coward, but that was an impersonal fight, and I had no inspiring rage; and should someone attack me in the bar I'd dislike it but I wouldn't run. It's war between neighbors, friends, relatives, and husbands and wives that I hate to see. Such war is rooted in love, thus the precursory words are the apter to become blows and shots. I want not to know of it, to be away. Violence puts me out of myself. That old skirmish at the Revland table had been shaking my thoughts when the Malmlunds arrived, and now the bad feeling was around me in the present. Twenty-four hours ago, Helmer Nelson had been killed. I shut the switchboard and doused the lamp and waited, Jake's mad aria still ringing in my head.

But the performance would not resume. It was as though the needle had stuck on *I! am! Villy! Sadness*! I must have intuited the developing of the Malmlund act and been holding to Jensine's request: the slamming of the screendoor did not at all surprise me. In an instant I had an eye to the window. Ida was backing in the direction of the car, some long object—a knife?—in her hand, and Paal was pursuing hesitantly. He had stripped to his shorts and his bare feet didn't like the gravel. The children were not in sight.

You touch me again and you'll be sorry! Ida snarled like a trapped wild thing. *You can throw the cat aginst the wall and bully women and kids, but you sure can't stand up to a man! You drank too much and you just got whipped, and now you want to take it out on me*!

Yes, it was a large carving knife.

Paal was both truculent and imploring: *Ya, and you're a liar. Shit! You didn't even see what happened! Put down that there thing and behave—I'm asking you.*

You let me alone! I've had enough! I'm simply going out on a drive, and if I drive into the Wild Rice River and it's the end of me, you can blame yourself! So don't you come an inch nearer!

No, no, Ida, that's craziness! And you don't even know how to drive.

She was within reach of his pale thin arm, but as he moved it she swung at him with the knife, an inept stroke. Dodging, Paal tripped and fell on his hands. *You sonofabitch coward*! she yelled. Ida made a blind dash to the car and started it and got it in low. Paal was on his feet again, chasing, an absurd naked shape in the night; and because of her inexperience, he was able to catch up and jump onto the left running board and grab for the ignition key. The motor died and the vehicle rolled to a stop, but the headlights stayed on. They were arguing, Ida behind the wheel and Paal sticking to the door, and I couldn't make out the words. I heard the engine again. Paal hopped off, extracting his arm in a hurry; she must have been raising the window. Then it was the boy Pete I saw. He ran from the house hollering *don't do it, Mom* and threw himself on the gravel in front of the car. The lights went out and the sound of the motor quit, and Ida was kneeling by her son, the two of them crying; and as she held him and walked him to the house, Paal following like a hangdog, I knew that the act was over. *That's okay, that's okay, Pete*, she kept saying, *we're not going to do this anymore, Pete, that's okay*. Arvid's is right across the main drag, and there was a lamp burning upstairs. Hedmark will have another new thing to talk about. The Malmlunds won't have to live it down, though; they've forced themselves to leave.

Ida Iverson had been a solemn girl, not too pretty, not too plain. Her sister Bee had inherited O. H.'s sarcasm, her brothers O. H.'s aggressiveness (though they're men of work, not the word), but Ida had gotten her personality from the earnest, unassuming Jensine. It was not that Jensine and her tribe were incapable of rage, just that, unlike the Iversons, they didn't show it in public. They might have been devils at home, Jensine as wroth as Jake Revland, who was also thought to be demure; I can't say. I can say that I was shocked. If it's hard to imagine Paal angry, Ida with a knife in her hand is a sight to disbelieve. She seemed possessed. Perhaps she was, and Bob Rustad too, both of them the tools of a malignance that has been accumulating in the rooms and minds of the township and can no longer stay hid, or perhaps it is the times demanding all that was private to come out. In either case, nobody would be unaffected. I'd have to watch myself.

But I wouldn't need to call Jensine. The boy's melodramatic move had chastened Ida and Paal, and now they could only sleep. I thought I'd do the same; the late drinking should have prepared me. Once I got into the bathroom, however, I realized that my own day was not at an end. The man in the mirror looked tried but not tired. Since I was going to watch myself, I might as well shave.

This bathroom was among the first in the township. I installed it so that Ben wouldn't have to go out to the *earth-closet*, and it has a stool, a sink, a tub, a medicine rack—everything except hot water. The cold is pumped up from a basement cistern linked to the well Uncle Ted dug. To bathe, we must heat water in buckets. The shaving we used to leave to Erik Rustad. I'd visit his shop every morning, and in the evening he'd come and do Ben right here. *My, you have a nice growt*, he'd coo. *I yust got hair on da lip and da tip of da chin. Even my beard ain't vert much*. Erik's death was an inconvenience. No one replaced him. A haircut, rare necessity, could be had in Nora; or Art Engstrom could give one cheap. But a lot of men had patronized Erik so long that they'd forgotten how to shave themselves. It was Arvid, putting in a stock of electric razors, who averted a local renaissance of the beard. If I was a somewhat reluctant purchaser, Ben was not. He must have known he'd fall in love with the gnawing gadget; I've heard him singing to its buzz. I detested the thing for its touch and its sound and its very handiness—the electric razor is as ingressive as television— but I didn't acknowledge the source of my hatred until tonight. Had I chosen to shave myself wet, I still would have had to look in the mirror. This is what I wanted to avoid. Two womanless fellows inhabiting a place, and one of them purblind, don't have much need of mirrors. In 1921 I took down those Ma had used, and Ben said nothing. Between then and the time of Erik's suicide, I managed to live without seeing my reflection—without reflection, period. But now, each day, the razor shrilling, I had to meet the eyes of Villy Sadness. I took off my shirt and squinted into them, and at him. The harsh light, coming from above, accentuated the wrinkles and made the nose and the brow seem prominent, and the thin-lipped mouth was grave indeed. My hair had been so pale brown that its etiolation in middle age was almost unnoticeable; at least I'd kept it. The eyes themselves were in shadow, the sockets skull-like. *Surprising he didn't remarry, such a handsome guy*, people are supposed to have said. But they mustn't have been talking about the presence in the mrror. This Villy had a drab face. The body was an even more ignored thing. Mine had never been sick or hurt or starved or overfed, Ben's meals having saved it that once (or I could have drunk it to death), and years of exercise had trimmed and toned it so that I didn't know it was there. A good animal, I thought, as I studied the lean, grey-haired chest and the muscled arms and the unsagging stomach, but it's sad. It wasn't just I who'd been ignoring my body. No one else had looked at it, put a caring hand on it, either, not since her death: I had gone celibate. There was the face again, tried, dispassionate, white stubble showing. It was very sad. I had hated shaving and the gadget that went with it because I didn't want to see what only my love had seen.

I shelved the razor. Ben could wait to hear his favorite electric song in the morning. I pulled the light-cord and went groping (like Ben at midday) to the bedroom, and now I'm supine in the dark and the throbbing is faint but steady. The liquor's exhausted; it didn't help.

Wine may have helped Jake Revland, but those nearest him bore the expense. I wonder how he saw the *handsome guy* at his table—as a threat? Perhaps he didn't hate me at all but thought I had the makings of an ideal stooge; perhaps his ire was fabricated. I did keep to the reactive role in that first turn of ours. Had I challenged him, worse scenes might not have ensued. But I was too surprised to strike back, *and you were there, Ingeborg.*

Someone had to get mad, however, and when Jake spilled wine, it was Selma. *That'll do*, she said, jumping up. *You've ruined the meal anyway, your arrogant talking and stuff—now this. Ingeborg, we've got to clear and take the things in the kitchen and soak the tablecloth, or it'll be a mark. My gracious*

He wasn't ready to quit. Ingeborg's attempt to leave the table provoked him. *You sit where you are!*

Don't listen to that nonsense, Ingeborg. Selma was gathering dishes. *Come on and bring the roast.*

But Ingeborg stayed. She had yet to lift her eyes or speak.

I can lend you a hand, I told my mother-in-law.

You sit there, too! Prefer not to drink with the Revland family, is that it, Mr. Nameless? Well, that's your choice, and you've spoiled the evening. But you're going nowhere until you've accounted for your actions!

Jake raised his no longer brimming glass in a mock skaal and drained it. I said nothing, but I was mad now; he'd involved Ingeborg. That was the time to quell him. Before I could think of a word, Selma darted in and seized the bottle.

If we have to throw out good food, we can throw this, and you're not having another drop! She ran to the kitchen and started pouring the wine into the slop bucket.

He tried to follow as quickly, but his legs were mutinous; he missed the door. *Go downstairs, Mrs. Revland!* he shouted, braced against the wall he'd hit. *Go downstairs or I will! And you*—Jake shook a finger at his straight man—*you just sit where you are!*

When his back left the room, Ingeborg whispered *Villy* and the two of us escaped by the front way. It was growing night, the air thick and purple. We crossed the yard, not touching as we would have done, and walked in silence to an outlying granary. The distant shouts were continuous. I asked if Selma would need us in there.

She can manage him, said Ingeborg, her tone brittle.

The west side of the granary, not visible from the house, had a door with a large rock step. There isn't much stone in the old lakebed valley, but once in a while an erratic's uncovered and must be dug out, or, if it's too big, worked around. This was but man-sized, and the original settler, dragging it onto the stead, may have had in mind the use to which Jake would put it—or even Ingeborg and I. That rock became our fugitive seat, its density preserving us as it did the warmth of the now set sun. It's still where it lay, no doubt.

Ingeborg was sobbing, face hidden, and I responded. When a loved wife cries, one holds her. She wouldn't talk, though, and I supposed the talking was mine to do and a part of the comforting. What emerged was the resentment I had not let myself voice.

He's something, that dad of yours. I couldn't believe it. Oh, he can hate me and say whatever he wants, but I won't put up with him insulting you and your mother. Don't feel too bad—you didn't do anything to him I could see. He was inventing the whole situation. Why, I don't know. Sometimes I wish you'd tell me more about him, so I could understand. I've never seen a man act like that. He was almost inhuman! Well, there's the drinking; you told me and you were right. God, he must have been at it half the afternoon! Most people can drink and enjoy themselves, but not that guy. It's not your fault, Ingeborg, and I went on, repeating the same words in various bitter combinations, hugging my wife who did not speak until I'd argued myself into a rage and was proposing to *go and give him a lesson in new world courtesy and if he objects, I'll kick him outside and see how he likes that.*

No, you mustn't. You could as well strike me. I'd expected the crying to have softened her, but the tautness hadn't changed. Ingeborg put her hand on mine and withdrew it. She seemed confused.

I was annoyed. *How should I deal with him then? Sit there and take it? I indulged him tonight, but once is enough. That kind of behavior is noxious. Don't you agree? Selma doesn't tolerate him.*

It's not so simple. Ingeborg was leaning back on the granary door, her breathing arrhythmic.

I don't claim it's simple. Perhaps your dad is sick in body or mind, unable to restrain himself, and I understand how you feel. I can because I love you. But something has to be done. I wouldn't think you'd ask me, the man you love, to listen to insults the rest of our time here. I sure hope you wouldn't.

Yes, I love you, she said, the tears and a shade of our old intimacy returning; and she returned my embrace also, gripping me hard. *I love him and you both, and I wish I knew what to suggest. It was just agonizing—Papa's never been this ill! He was awful to you, Villy, I know that and I wanted to die; but it's the sickness. We have to find a way of avoiding it is all. Only nine short months and it'll be spring, then we'll have a place of our own.*

The gibbous moon had been up a while, but I didn't look at it until we quit our rock and entered the haymeadow. Its saffron tint marked harvest, a term of content, of plenty. Ingeborg's hair was alight. Down towards the river, a dog was barking—perhaps at some fieldhand on the trek to Nora—and that was the one sound. Waking from distress and to such a sweet, warm world, we could think ourselves happy again. We *were* better. Jake would be collapsing and Selma hauling him to bed, she knew, and we hadn't too much of an exile to wait out; so we walked and talked of our new home and even laughed a little. This was our young *way of avoiding*.

Selma had left a candle and a tray of sandwiches in the kitchen. The other rooms were dark. We took the food upstairs and ate, then went whispering to bed. It was like the nocturnal escapades of childhood. What would happen next, I asked her.

You'll see, don't worry.

Should I try and stay clear of him?

You won't have to.

For almost a week, he did not show up in the yard or in the fields or at the table. He'd been so *ill* that his recovery was protracted and kept him to the bedroom. I had enough to do with plowing and the livestock, but Jake's help I didn't miss; I too had things to get over. Yet one's adaptive bent is strong. It seemed right to let myself be guided by the women, to accept him as an invalid. The house became an infirmary, and I was made to hush while in it; they had assumed the austere solicitude of nurses. Even before Selma talked to me, I had come to believe Jake *sick* and more a victim than a culprit. She appeared in the barn one morning, a mug of coffee in her hand, her eyes dispirited.

Oh, Villy, I brought you this. It was odd hearing someone there. *You didn't even get a cup at breakfast, poor boy, and such work you've been doing! I must apologize. We're all out of kilter these days, you know—hard keeping up with the chores and the garden and the cooking, and then he has to be fed separate. If you and Ingeborg weren't here, we'd never manage. You drink this now. I finally got the second pot made, though how I found the time —*

It's good of you. I smiled and took off my gloves; I'd been cleaning a stall. She might have said what she had thus far in the presence of others. That was where she always seemed to be, visiting, entertaining (when Jake was not around), going to Ladies' Aid; and at night she had us. If I liked Selma, everyone did. But she and I had not conversed alone, and as I sipped the morning gift I must have been aware of her intention.

I wanted to explain to you about the other night. She patted my arm as though to forestall me. *Ingeborg may have mentioned something, but this problem he's got is new and she loves her papa and it's all bewildering to her so I thought I'd tell you.*

Is he doing all right?

Selma sniffed. *Hah, he could have been up the next day! He's just being timid and hoping we forget. Mr. Revland didn't use to be like this, Villy; he was always kind and churchgoing and educated, and he never, never approved of drinking. I was a mere country girl and they said I was fortunate to get such a gentleman. Well, that was true. He's proud and doesn't take to a lot of visitors — and me, I enjoy people, heavensakes — but he didn't start in with the wine till a couple of years ago. I guess it's my fault. We made wine at home long's I can remember and that was served at big occasions, holidays and such, and no one drank excessive. I'd no idea Mr. Revland was to get sick on it. I spose I'll have to stop making, that's all.*

Ya, some it doesn't agree with. I stood there bland and dignified, trying to seem the gentleman he no longer was.

I think he's allergic and it changes him and he gets wild. I read in a magazine where allergies can do that to you. Oh, he hasn't raised a hand to me or others; that's not his way. But he can sure get vicious talking. I don't know if I should give it back to him or what. Villy — she patted me again and looked dead earnest — *I'm ashamed how he treated you, and you did well not answering him as he deserved. You had real gumption. I thank the stars our Ingeborg has you; I wanted to tell you that. I know with you on the place we can survive.*

Let's hope he doesn't have another spell.

She glanced out the barn window to where the house sat waiting. *I pray and pray he doesn't. I must run in — Mr. Revland has to have me nearby. But, Villy, there was something else I wanted to say: if it happens, just be calm and don't get mad or leave. We'll cure him with patience and trusting in God. I know it would break Ingeborg's heart to go away and her papa sick, and I'd feel bad too, so please don't leave.* Selma gave me a quick hug in parting. *I wish I had more to advise you. I'm sorry. You're a good young man.*

I was pleased. She had meant to enlist me but in fact had strengthened my case. Flattering that *good young man*, she'd endued him with power and in time he'd wield it. Selma couldn't have known then that she was rushing the downfall of all she'd sought to preserve; I was just as ignorant. The pleasure came of Jake's reduction in status. Now he had been ruled *wrong* as well as *sick*, I wouldn't have to conciliate him.

We should have moved out at once. I didn't need avengement. If we had, Selma's counsels might have wrought the intended healing. Yes, we should have taken a room in Hedmark or somewhere, spent no more than work days on the farm, kept distant and polite; the new home would have been ready soon enough. But we didn't leave, and those *nine short months* have yet to pass. I wonder if Selma's mourned what might have been. The Revlands died, to me, at the death of Ingeborg so I've had no chance to ask. In 1930, when a stroke killed Jake, she sold the farm to Pete Johannesson and went to their sister's in Minneapolis; she's having a hale late life, I understand. Should I write Selma tomorrow, say I'm the one who's sorry?

I didn't plan to retaliate, though; I was feeling too wise and superior. In The Reemergence of the Invalid, an entr'acte performed next to the windmill, I had a tricky part and handled it. I'd been up to uncrook a blade and seen him approaching as I descended, the Jake of old, an aristocratic walker in the morning. *Just seem like it didn't happen*, they'd coached, and I'd had days to practice. It would be smart, I knew, to give him the opening line.

Hello there. You fixed that blade, eh? He must have had the same coach. I detected no embarrassment or rankling in him; Jake was again the civil personage. These were not the eyes of *the other night*. All that belied him was a scrape on his forehead.

Ya, the storm bent it worse. I was plowing when it began, so I didn't get back to stop the wheel right away.

I unlocked the wheel and we stood a minute gawking upward.

It's lucky we didn't have to replace it, he said. *One must send to Chicago, and orders are a month in coming.*

I took it out and pounded it flat. I think it should do.

You did the job at the top of the mill, eh? That was daring. I have no head for heights.

The wheel spun evenly, the metal cock above it pointing northwest. I wondered about the scrape. He must have fallen and hit himself late that night; it hadn't been there when Ingeborg and I withdrew. Or perhaps Selma had used a stick to *manage him.*

How's Noah's eye? The big draft horse had injured it in the stall. He and Adam, his aging partner, had been heroic on the early farm, pulling all that men couldn't budge; now they were used to take grain wagons out of the field—just to the yard, no longer to town—and in occasional rescue and moving work, but their great times had ended. Both Jake and I liked the horses and would separately visit them. We hadn't discussed this. But I knew that in his mention of Noah, he was also referring to our private common sympathy.

I haven't looked at it, but he's acting fine. The vet was supposed to check on it this morning and remove the bandage, that's why I was waiting around here. Otherwise I'd be out on the north twenty.

Well, I could always see to Noah. He consulted his pocket watch. *If you wanted to go ahead, you might be able to finish by noon.*

With the twenty? Oh yes, and that'll be the last of the plowing.

Excellent, said Jake, smiling as he started off, his arm raised in archaic valediction. *I'll watch for the vet and take care of some other things. Nice of you to fix the blade. We'll see you at lunch!* That arm gesture was soon to be revived by Mussolini.

I was still part kid, part man and believed in human good nature—what I'd learned in Russia seemed remote as the place itself—so following our little dialogue, I'd have been prepared to make truce. If *he* wanted it, I'd sign; and I thought he did. His flattery had worked. It had relieved me of my apprehensiveness. When I stopped for lunch, I could tell that Selma too was disburdened. She was no more knowing than I in the labyrinth of human ways and didn't see that Jake had managed to lull his opponent without giving an inch: he hadn't said my name.

Best to end it there at the table, chitchat humming and hopes reviving and Ingeborg pouring coffee, end it or leave the page unturned. Why read the latter acts? I was in them. I wish I could sleep. But Ingeborg's so close now, I'm reminded of the light that interspersed the tragedy, the part I hadn't dared recall; and this is why I'm awake. I wonder if it did end that autumn. Perhaps I'm *living* act six. I must go on to a day that could have been our summit (and ignore its well-remembered evening while I can); I'll find her there. It was around equinox, the greens of the country swelling, that Ingeborg and I drove out to the Lindgren farm. We'd have much to do in restoring it and wanted to make a joint appraisal. The idea of a home in the woods had been Ingeborg's, but I wasn't hard to sway; and Selma became our agent and talked Pete into letting us rent the stead without the tillage. What Jake thought, we didn't know. But I doubted he would object, since I'd be working on the house in the fall and winter and should be done by planting. *Or did you know? There were things you withheld, Ingeborg.* The Lindgrens' was unfenced then, no gate or cattle, and we parked in the tall grass of the yard and sat a moment and looked at our future dwelling. They'd left only thirteen years back, so the paint wasn't gone but tarnished and most of the shingles seemed all right. The interior would be the main job. We'd do that first and move in, then I'd tend to the roof (which might be leaky) and the outside walls. It would be nothing to clear the yard in spring, the old growth dead and the new just up; and she'd be starting a garden. Uncle Pete had kept the well active. We sat and looked and figured, huge bees droning in the tinted warmth of Mrs. Lindgren's persistent hollyhocks, the wild greens richening, Ingeborg in a light dress, hair unbound, and we went on talking as we inspected the void, murky rooms of the house, visioning what we'd do in each of them—piano and bookshelves here, the guest bed there—and as we strolled through the yard to lay claim to the outbuildings. The summer kitchen needed windows and Pete had razed the barn, but we'd have the big vacant granary to put a cow and horses in, and it wouldn't take me long to build a coop. We were in accord, not just on practical things, but all: she too was one for reclusion in nature, was delighted with the vast wood and pasture land we'd have to ourselves. The whole place would be our garden.

It's so perfect, Villy, she said, and I can see her now, a stalk of grass between her lips. *I think it was meant to be our home, don't you? I dreamt of it when I was little, after Mama took me with to see the Lindgrens; and I always wanted to come back. There wasn't anywhere as quiet. I can't wait till spring.*

There won't be much quiet once the hammering starts, said the lucky idiot I was. Away from her parents, Ingeborg would change to a

meditative grownup and speak of high matters, music and books and solitude, but I, caught in my role, found the switch awkward and would continue prattling to her like a workman. Distress would snap me out, or merrymaking, and I'd turn my full self; otherwise, we'd have to be alone a while before I could. Those days I didn't know that I was living under such constraint. He had the both of us acting.

We stood at the edge of the yard, the pasture sloping eastward to the distant riverwoods, the grass so thick that only the few isolated oaks had been able to top it, and watched a show of white and orange butterflies. *Pete hasn't hayed yet*, I said. *I'll ask to do a part of the mowing, then maybe he'll let us have some next year. Lindgren must have left these oaks. They couldn't have sprung up since.*

You know what it reminds me of? said Ingeborg, oblivious to my banality. *Grandma's painting of the meadow in Sweden, the one she brought along on the boat. It used to hang in the dining room, but I think Papa got tired of it. You must see that painting—the landscape is just like this, lone oaks and everything, and no people. Let's go down to the river. Is it far?*

Well, I was supposed to help Ben today, too.

But Ingeborg was chasing the butterflies, dwindling into the scene that Selma's Swedish mother had recorded, and when at last I saw the painting Ingeborg was in it, a white whit, perhaps a slip of the brush or an attempted sunbeam in the dark woods' beginning, appreciable only to one who was there and should have been there on the night she ran all the way. I would find the painting in the boxes of things Selma was to send; I'd burn it with the photos and the rest. Best to leave her there, calling to me from the end of the meadow, leave her in the time that's turned to ash. *Come on, Villy, I'm inside the painting!* I obeyed her then, made a panic charge through the hot grass as the speck that was Ingeborg fled into shade, but to do so now (and I can hear the words) would mean reliving the discovery—no, the ambush: Ingeborg sitting in a burdock jungle, pretending hurt, one knee raised to rub her calf; burrs on her dress and her full white thighs in view, the mole that always aroused me and a thrush singing; *and you waited until I knelt to see what was wrong, then laughed and put your legs around my neck and rolled; we hadn't done it out of the house before, and it had been secretive, almost spiritual, your parents maybe listening; but in the woods that afternoon, we did it like two freed savages, possessing the earth as we took each other*; and no, I can't go on; such closeness is unrelivable; to join her in the painting now I'd have to turn to ash myself.

Time is nothing. Place is the one preservative of memory; what was seen and smelt and touched abides in it. There's no remembering without some place, and all place is given. Words are but a continual revising of time, a shield, an essay, a lecture, news. I've needed them. I'm not afraid of what was said—it's been changed—but Ingeborg didn't exist in words; she belonged to a place. She's still there where she chose to be and die and my description of it unstills her, and were I able to accept that choice I'd let it alone. It is because I avoided the place that I've never understood Ingeborg. I can barely recall the gist of our talk as we disentwined and picked off the burrs and the bugs and walked satiate into the meadow, the light stroking us; our words were languid.

How late is it? she said.
Two o'clock, who knows?
And you were to go to your brother. We're disgusting.
I'll just have to tell him.
I bet you would. I thought of someone else: Uncle Pete comes over every day. What if he saw us like this?
Or your parents?
Well, I have a comb along.

She stopped me in the yard, her eyes teasing and afire. *Let's stay, Villy. If I wanted you again, right now, to be sure and make a child, I know I could get you to do it.* She began lifting her dress, but when I moved, she retreated. *Think of your brother, Villy, and my uncle!*
I am.

It was all game. We laughed ourselves serious, then went to the car and drove, and as we approached the Revland farm the quieter we kept. We should have stayed in our garden. Ingeborg must have been wishing it. But I was brooding on a thing said, the child: that's the gist I recall.

I dropped her at the Revlands' and continued into town, where the company had need of my services. A branch had fallen onto one of the poles, so I'd have to strap on the hooks and go up and saw it. Ben was a grunt, of course, and I did much of the elevated work; linemen from Bell would help with resagging and other momentous jobs. It was about such a job I was thinking, and when I'd completed my acrobatics—a simple stunt and all he had for me that day—I told him that I'd like to string wire to the Lindgrens'. I couldn't do it, or ask Bell, myself; the request would have to be made by the company. We had no pole gins or pike poles or crew, thus the setting would have taken *us* a month, and I wanted the poles set before the ground froze so I'd have but to string the line in April. Ben nodded. We both knew that the farm had to be connected, else he couldn't reach me. The note I wanted him to cosign would be for a piddling amount; I had banked my share of Jake's crop. *You're keeping aside enough to work on the house?* was Ben's one query. I was, and we struck the deal and sat chatting into the afternoon. I'd meant to get back to Revlands' and mow, but it was nice talking; he and I had done little of it through the marriage summer. Old Mrs. Svensgaard was a good employee, though Ben had detected some gossip—*and she's Ma's age*, he said, chuckling. *Now you'll be here again, I can send her home.* I was lazing in the residues of amorousness and enjoying our quiet powwow and it was hot, the last wave of the season, and I thought the chair would never let go. It must have been almost five when Ingeborg called.

Villy, she whispered, not quite like a ladylove, but she didn't sound mad. *There's something you should know.*

Are people sleeping?

No, listen: Papa's been downstairs. Mama has him in their room, though, and he's getting better. I hope he'll be all right by mealtime.

How did the attack—

I must hang up. I want you to come to the table anyway and pretend there's nothing, but you should ready your patience. That's all.

Sure I'll come. What are you doing?

I might play piano, he likes that so much.

In 1930, with Jake dead, there was to be a second call and whispered name. The instant I heard *Villy* I believed it was Ingeborg and that it had all been a mistake or a deception and she'd returned to apologize and settle things. I couldn't respond. *This is Tina*, she continued. *I've got laryngitis.* Ingeborg's low, hymning voice was distinctive but her articulation like that of others in the neighborhood, as whispering betrayed. Tina would never know the shock—how, for a roseate instant, there'd been magic in the telephone.

I headed towards Revlands' thinking, *to be sure and make a child.* We hadn't talked of having one or not. I doubt I had dreamed it; to my mind, children simply occurred; and that was and is the mind of rural North Dakota, where the idea of having a choice in the matter has yet to arise. Now, looking back, I'd say that we wouldn't have needed a baby to complete us. We were a whole together. Then, I was speculating: perhaps Ingeborg's already pregnant (we had had four months and more) and her teasing a way of telling. I wouldn't object. I was in a honeymoon startle, and the thought of fathering had charm and dominated me on the slow trip to the Revlands', so I managed to forget what she'd said of Jake. At least I wasn't consciously wary of him as I entered the house, but I arrived well in time. The piano allayed the atmosphere. Ingeborg was doing selections from *La Traviata*, memento of our courtship, Jake resting with a mug in his hand; he looked more tired than sick. There was little to alarm one, though Selma had shot me a glance in the entry.

Ingeborg stood up, neat and reserved once again and not the sort who'd climb into a painting or lift her dress or tussle in the burdock. No, this was a lady of culture.

Beautiful, said Jake, *oh wasn't it beautiful?* He seemed straining to show how moved he was. I could see no imp in his eyes; they were moist, however, and he was holding the coffee mug at a tilt.

She smiled. *Thank you. I put out a clean shirt for you, Villy, if you'd like to change and so forth. It's on the bed. Mama should have supper soon.*

As I walked up the stairs, I heard Jake resuming: *The concert isn't over, is it? I was hoping you'd play some Grieg, you know the one*; and then the piano indulging him.

He's still drunk, I thought. There were three stages of drunkenness, beginning with the jovial and the malevolent, and he had passed into the whiny third stage and would be less of a threat to us than to himself. I'd become an expert watching the doughboys, a lot of whom had gone beyond stage three to coma, and I had found the drinking men of Hedmark to be the same. I took the shirt and socks and underthings and went to the bath house and did a leisurely toilet; the all-knowing don't have to rush. Jake would adhere to pattern. In fact, he did. But I was to learn that while one man's mind may work like another's, what's in it is different.

The mood at the wineless table was too relaxed, Jake blear and Selma drawn and Ingeborg and I in pleasant hebetude. Our eating in the dining room—and again the best cloth was spread, the old silver and china set—would have fazed me earlier, but now I didn't even ask why we were celebrating. Jake said grace in both *norsk* and English, adding a plea that God *bless the soul of her, the departed, to whom we owe so much*, and he choked on *amen*. No pretoast cathechizing subverted the meal this time.

Villy must not have been told, said Selma in an obituary voice. *Did you mention it, Ingeborg? Well, this is the birthday of Mr. Revland's mother—or it would have been. She lived in Norway and never did get to visit us in America.*

Ingeborg turned to me without looking up. *Yes, we always observe the day.* Jake remained bowed, a picture of mourning, till his wife should caption it; he wanted to fix it in our minds.

My condolences, I said, unsure of the word's propriety.

Oh, she's been gone a while. Selma was discreet in handing the food around. *I think it's all of sixteen years. That's right—exactly. She was a real distinguished person, you know, and I wish we'd had a chance to meet her, Ingeborg and I.*

She was a religious person, said Jake. The circulating bowls had roused him but he was thick-tongued and his head stayed bent. *It was she that taught us the meaning of sinfulness. Just as well she didn't come to America. She would not have approved of this land.*

She was very pure, very religious, Selma said to me; like Ingeborg, she didn't raise her eyes. *It made her so glad we were married in the Norwegian church, I remember. And you saw what she sent Ingeborg, that nice little Bible? That was quite a gift.*

I said I had and thought it was very nice. But I'd gotten absorbed in eating. Jake had no attention to spare us anyway. He was visioning a someone else, an otherwhere:

She was a beautiful person who understood the dangers of beauty. I sailed with her to visit my aunt in Haugesund, and I must have been a young, young kid, and just the two of us went, Bergen to Haugesund, and we sailed through the fjords and along the sea and it was clear and there were nothing but beautiful mountains rising above, and so I said to her, Mother, isn't it beautiful? That's all I said. We were out on the deck and, you know, she just stared at me and took me inside and then she said, You must blind yourself to all that perishes and see only the light of God. That's what she said. You must blind yourself to all that perishes and see only the light of God.

I hadn't heard his *norsk* accent before; his good English must have been wine-soluble. Now he paused to use a handkerchief. I felt almost sympathetic towards him and thought I'd do a bit of encouraging: *She sounds like quite a religious person, your mother.*

She was a distinguished person who understood the meaning of sinfulness and taught the dangers of beauty. Jake had had to work, but at last the language was obeying him. *She was too good for this world. I know she was too good for the homeland because I heard the ridicule. It's as well she didn't come to America; they would have laughed at her here. When I departed, it was like an amputation and she was so hurt she couldn't even talk until the moment I was to sail. Then she gave me the most beautiful thing she had, her wisdom. Seek out the wretched, she said, seek out the wretched and trust in their company.* He sobbed into the handkerchief. *Excuse me, everyone!*

Selma hastened to interpret. Her eyes were up this time, and embarrassed. *You see, Villy, Mr. Revland was close to his mother. She used to write him once a week without fail, but at the end—*

Excuse me, said Jake, suddenly out the kitchen door, his face averted.

She let a few seconds pass. *Go ahead and eat*, she said in an undertone. *He's always like this on her birthday. You're doing just fine. And since he started—oh no!* Selma had noticed or thought of something and was off in pursuit.

What's the crisis? I winked at Ingeborg but she missed it.

Please don't joke, Villy. He was awful this afternoon when I got back, loud and arrogant, and now he's trying to go to the cellar again. There's a creak in the third step and that was what Mama—oh if only he'd recover!

Thinking she meant to silence me, I directed my attention to the food. It was delicious: potatoes and meatballs and rutabaga. I could hear Selma's voice scolding below. Then they returned to the table, Selma sapped but Jake a little steadier. Maybe he'd gotten a nip before she caught him. *You're right, you're right*, he was mumbling as he sat down and located his fork, *all we can do is live.* I was the image of nonchalance; easy to be patient with this patient.

While a drinking man cannot revert from stage to stage, I liked to theorize, a solid meal may mitigate the stage he's in. Time and Selma's cooking had bolstered Jake. Soon he'd sleep or bcome hung over. Meanwhile he was drunk, his maudlinness fortified. As he spoke, he seemed more aware of our existence than he'd been. *One must live, she says, and it's true. Live while one can and seek out the wretched—*

how else to survive in the valley of the shadow of death? You're right, Mrs. Revland, and that was her very advice, the same words. She knew I was sailing into heathendom, into the land of the fatted calf, she said, and I would need heavenly guidance. I remembered. By God, I remembered! But it was years of seeking till I sought out the wretched, so long it took to find a man of purity. Oh, we can laugh at him now! In those days, let me tell you, he was a regular saint. I thought I had found a saint.

Yes, Helmer was an outstanding young man, said Selma, *and never swore and stuff like that.*

This was *news* indeed: *You were friends to Helmer Nelson?*

My yes, we saw him every week. He'd come and read the Bible with Mr. Revland.

I didn't know.

We can laugh. Jake filled his mouth so that the audience had to wait for him to swallow. *Most young people are atheists now, but at the time we met there was but one in the whole township—and he went into law, of course. No, this young fellow was outstanding. Mrs. Revland's right. He stood out even among the pious, that's how outstanding he was, let me tell you. He was pure and taught the meaning of sinfulness—and this was a handsome lad the girls watched. If it hadn't been that one flaw in his thinking, who can say? So when we laugh we should remember the kind of man he might have been.*

It must have been 1905 he stopped visiting, said Selma to me, but I saw she'd tired of the topic. *He and Mr. Revland didn't get along so well anymore.*

Either Jake's spurt had ended or he was pretending to sink. He became whiny again, wheedling. *Didn't I try my best to show him the way? He was a saint and a beautiful person and yet he wouldn't acknowledge the truth. It was so simple: one may be saved by grace alone. What's hard about that? I explained it and explained it, as Mother had done with me: one-may-be-saved-by-grace-alone. But nossir, he said, salvation has to be earned by deeds. Deeds? How can an evil man perform good deeds, I asked, and there I had him. He actually believed that people are good at heart. Such pride ill behooves the wretched. I had to admit that I could no longer trust in his company. I loved that young guy, you know.*

Too spent to cry, he could only sit chin on chest and sniffle. Selma watched him; Ingeborg and I watched our empty plates. For the three of us the meal was over, and myself, I was sick of listening.

Well, thanks, I said to Selma, *I enjoyed the supper.*

She smiled with relief and some pain. *You're most welcome. It was nothing. Ingeborg, would you help and clear the table? I'll tend to the dishes.*

Jake raised a weak hand. *I have one request*, he said, talking into his lap. *It's not much and will take but a minute. I'd like us all to join in prayer for the soul of the deceased, the young people too. I ask that the young people set aside their atheism in memory of her soul. Come, I beg you.*

He lurched up and dragged his chair away from the table. *See, this is the altar. Come, let us kneel by it.*

Both Selma and Ingeborg were tight-lipped but nodding at me, and Jake had slumped into position. I knew I couldn't go along with this. I'd always believed in God and at twenty-one I believed in the church as well, but I'd had my fill of Jake that evening; his notion seemed grotesque, sacrilegious. Be patient, they'd said. I was enduring his melodrama, hiding what I really felt, and *no one* could expect more of me.

Let us pray, he whined, elbows on the chair, *I'm begging you.*

I stood to prepare my exit. I would leave civilly, but I'd leave. *This is not my kind of drill*, I said, *and you'll have to excuse me now.*

The women did a wild pantomime to halt me, beckoning, imploring, but I was set on my way. Ingeborg's lips said *Villy* and there was a dark fright in her I'd never seen; as I marched upstairs and lay in our bed, I thought of that.

Jake's trials with Helmer must have occurred around 1910, so I wouldn't have heard of them. Even in time, I was to hear nothing beyond what I learned in the Revland house. The two were naturally reticent; Jake wasn't a man to publicize his homelife, and to Helmer the subjective didn't avail; so the township were kept in ignorance. Their struggle might have had a different outcome. Perhaps, had he allowed that *one may be saved by grace alone*, it would have been Helmer Nelson marrying Ingeborg. The news that he's been shot is more upsetting than it should be.

I lay in bed an hour, aggrieved but thinking of Ingeborg's strange look, and downstairs the stirrings were few and muted. The bathetic ceremony could *not* go on all night. Jake *had* to have quit. I wanted her next to me. There was so much penned in both of us. All sound stopped a minute and I felt she was approaching; then came the clink of dishes in water. I hissed an army expression. She belonged with *me*, not the dishes. Selma had said she'd tend to them. But Ingeborg entered the room at last and took a chair by the window, and I saw her profile in the dim as she sat gazing out—not at her husband. She seemed too aloof. By then, such was my annoyance, I didn't care.

You had no need or right to insult him, Villy, she said, her tone cold and flat.

I had been prepared to unbottle everything, to lose the resentment in loosing it, but this shocked me dumb. It wasn't *my* Ingeborg talking; this was an opponent. I'd engage her if she liked, but I wouldn't show a feeling. *I insulted nobody. How is one to treat a fool?*

Is it your father-in-law you're describing?

Who else?

I can't permit you to malign him, Villy.

And yet you'd permit him anything?

You'd better say no more.

I wish you would tell him that.

She paused, her breathing quick and loud. But her anger, like mine, was in check. *You seem to have no regard for him or me*, she said, rising. *I'll let you sleep alone tonight.*

This blew my cork and I was out of the bed and grabbing her, shaking her, yelling with no thought to the calm of the house. *You'll sleep where you belong! What's the matter with you, Ingeborg, are you blind and deaf? Don't you realize that he's making fools of us all? You're the one who has no regard—for your husband! You think so little of your husband that you insist I participate in a mockery and a sacrilege just to amuse a drunkard?*

I hear those past yellings, the past weepings too, and I wonder if it was wrong to nurse such hate against him. No doubt it was, though Jake's own wrong had sowed it; one should not repay bad in kind. But the hate existed and I yelled and Ingeborg was weeping, limp in my grip, then both of us were weeping and I was holding her gentle as I used to do, and we went to the bed and lay in each other's arms and it was Ingeborg's turn to try to speak it free.

The words issued hot on my neck. *I'm sorry. You're the dearest person in my life and I know I shouldn't have blamed you. I haven't been right since this afternoon—and we'd had such a wonderful time in the painting. He was terrible*! Another rush of tears, and I almost hoped that she wouldn't continue. But: *He saw me come in. I wasn't too tidy, you know. He was in the living room—and Mama out watering the trees—but he had been downstairs; I can recognize that insane smile. I was going to clean up and change, and he just planted himself in front of me and said, Is this how you celebrate your grandmother's birthday? We'd have to have a little conference, he said, a little conference, and he took and pushed me into their room and sat us on the bed and then he was asking—I'm not sure I should say the rest.*

I felt the wind leaving me and the hate returning, a killer-hatred. But I was to be strong now so I hid it. *I think you should.*

He made me tell, she said, tears constraining her voice.

Tell?

What we did in the woods! I had to describe it to him over and over and I was so ashamed. He stared at me something awful and then he said, Are you a couple of pigs that you rut in the bushes or are you children of God?

Your father said that?

I didn't know it was unnatural, Villy. But that's what he called it. Such unnatural practices are a terrible sin, he said. He even made me tell—

Yes?

—where you had put your hand. And as I told him, he'd put his hand there too, and he would say: Like this, eh? He wanted to judge the extent of our sinfulness. That man wasn't Papa, Villy. I wished I were dead. Please don't go.

I was out of the bed again, not yelling, however—pacing. Best to strangle him, I figured. In seconds I'd give him a real coma. A man like Bob Rustad would have been on the stairs already. Such I was not. But when I spoke I must have sounded as cold as she had earlier. *I understand. It was an act. He was afraid you'd told, that's why he pretended to be on his last legs. Do you see that? With him, everything's an act—the precious little illness, everything. I can be patient, but what he did to you this afternoon was wicked. And then he sits mewling of saints and purity. If he can treat you that way, his own child, you and I can move out. We're leaving tonight. We'll find rooms in Hedmark through the winter.*

The unbroken sobs of her reply were slow in slowing. They ceased eventually but she didn't talk; nor would I fill the moment. I watched and waited. *Come and hold me,* she said at length. *Hold me, for the love of God, and I'll do as you think we should.*

Thus we both began to accede. I was young enough and loved her enough to want rid of my anger, but it was still present. *I appreciate the concern you have*, I said reservedly. *He is your father and he may be sick—but it's a chosen illness. You and Selma can't help him. Perhaps he's got neurasthenia, like some of the men I saw in the army. If so, he should have medical treatment. In my opinion, though, he's just a drunk. I don't excuse him, and you and Selma mustn't either. Being patient is to encourage him. I love you, Ingeborg, and I respect myself. We can't stay here and be called pigs and with him violating your dignity, and that's that. So let's gather our possessions and I'll ring Art and he can drive us to Ben's place. We can sleep there a night at least.*

My touch had let Ingeborg collect herself. *You've tried so hard to be patient, Villy. Mama and I were wrong, and wrong to ask you; he's only gotten worse. I hope you can forgive. I'll do as you say and we'll move to town. But I want you to know how difficut it will be. I'm considering Mama. This trouble of his has weakened her spirit, and now she'll have to carry on alone, and Mama's not young anymore. I'm worried.*

Consider this, I said, weakening too but stubborn. *What if our absence cured him? It might be all he needs, a bit of solitude.*

It's possible. Who can say? Oh I wish you could have seen him when he was normal! Papa's so intelligent; he's got whole libraries in his brain. I can't believe he had this other side. I'll always love him. It's too bad and I want not to feel it. And next he'll probably kill himself or something.

The crying was lost, childlike; it originated in an old, old smart. Right then, I would have sold my soul to comfort Ingeborg. *If we did stay—a week or so, that is, to see how it went—if we stayed and he remembered this evening, well, perhaps he'd be more cautious. I did teach him a lesson.*

Her long soft arms tightened around my neck in gratitude, but her seriousness remained. That she'd been prepared to go with me, I had and have no doubt. She said: *It was well you didn't heed him, or us, that you kept your self-respect. You've taught him and you taught us too. But you have decided and for the best, I think, and it's mine to follow. I'm yours, Villy. Even if we did stay, it would be just so long as you wished; I wouldn't forget. And there's more I should have told you. Listen: as I was washing the dishes, Mama went and destroyed the wine. Not one drop left. So if we stayed, things might get better. He'll be shy of buying it.*

That pathetic conversation is easier to rehearse than our *rut in the bushes*. I've kept all that was sad and made a hermitic life of it. The words in which we mistook the world have always belonged to me; those of our light times, to Ingeborg. Will I ever say them?

Then, it seemed the talk had united us and that we'd be able to manage, and *manage him*, through the probationary weeks. Selma was not to be in on it. We would go about our jobs as though nothing had happened and be nice at supper and observe. I'd meanwhile see what rooms there were to rent, no more than that; I wouldn't take any. But, if Jake relapsed and we left, we'd have some notion of the whereto. He convalesced in hiding the whole first week and was served by nurses, and autumn came without incident. It was a smooth metamorphosis, the leaves finally assuming the hue of the earth, pending their drop to it, the weather cool and dry out of the northwest, weeds killed in a night, insects too, and smoke perfuming the air; and as I worked on the farm and in the Lindgren house, the sky's blue deepening, no Jake to deal with, I could imagine that our troubles had been part of the summer and so were fading. Selma was warm but somewhat autumnal in the eyes. She didn't bring me a morning cup or approach me alone, and when she spoke it was of business and the weather. It would be a short fall, Selma predicted; we'd have to put in extra hay. She was like someone who'd been so humiliated that she couldn't quite pardon the witnesses to it. I felt sorry and thought of going to her to ease things—I knew where she'd dumped the bottles, a wet patch at the edge of the north field, a touching site—but I was afraid I'd tell too much and thus I didn't. If Ingeborg respected the terms of our secret pact, and I could see she had, it was Villy set them and Villy's to be the exemplar of prudence. We two had chances to discuss it, in bed, on trips to our new home, but the reserve of that first week continued even after Jake was up and the test beginning and we might well have talked. Perhaps we wanted to make it thorough, try not just him but ourselves, *or perhaps in saying nothing we hoped to aid in time's effacement of the scene and of the quick unhappiness it brought, as though talking would have reified what otherwise had not occurred because it shouldn't have. I was scared. About you, Ingeborg, I don't know. We may have been close but I did not know about you. It wasn't only mine to be the exemplar of silence. You seemed content with the earth in your last full month upon it, your look, when you turned, revealing no doubt of yourself or me; I must have appeared the same. Untalking, we must each have believed the other steady. I don't mean the fear was conscious, or to overlook the many bright things there were to hold our minds that autumn, our planning and walking, the days' indigo, the loving that didn't need talk; I want to know if you were scared and realized it. We lived outwardly then, characters in a farm idyll who weren't meant to express or even have such knowledge, figurines in an Edenic diorama your parents had constructed and which you and I would inherit along with the hopes it embodied (unless we kept sinning), so I can't expect you to answer what I myself didn't know to ask: were you as strong as their dream? You would have fled to Hedmark that night and you joyed in the thought of moving to Lindgrens', but you were never tested away. You might soon have gone back to them. Was the Lindgrens' merely a placebo until we should be old and wise enough to accept the true garden of your childhood? Had we left, I could tell, but we stuck to our poses* and Jake and Selma to theirs. He let himself be seen one morning, a preoccupied distant man in black. I was oiling the hinges of the barn gate and quite visible, but he didn't come; there was no encore of our windmill intermezzo. Nor had the women advised me. *I think he'll be up* had been said, and in a tone suggesting that the news was unimportant. I worked that afternooon for the company and so had time to think. He'd be on stage again in the evening. I didn't dread it, though; he'd lost my respect and, with it, my interest. The battle was over. I'd only to observe him and pick the terms of the truce: to leave now or in the spring. As it was, he behaved himself, sitting there like a man just out of prison, one who'd wronged and been wronged, and his talk was subdued, inconsequential. The violinist Fremstad would be playing in Moorhead next month, he said, Selma encouraging him; that's all I remember. It wasn't fear of Jake I thought I experienced, it was contempt. Thus I masked my apprehension, half-knowing, at a deep, dirty level, what he must have known outright—that the war would continue.

I feared violence, not Jake's but that of the beast he roused in me, and living in a tableau that forbade it didn't help. I hated the man so much that my every small resentment, of Selma and Ingeborg too, and others, converged on him; yet speaking was also disallowed and I had to stay and be polite. A psychologist would describe those weeks as schizophrenic. They *are* nearly a blank. Oh I could repeat the burden of them and con the events—the setting of the poles, the early coming of winter, Ben breaking his thumb, the proclaiming of Armistice Day, Adam getting sick and Jake shooting him and then the tremendous gravedigging, and hammering in the cold in the Lindgren house, infrequently—but I'd have to deduce it all. Both that period and the time right after were caught in the circumgyration of a vortex, her death being its cavity, and things outside the normal flow are hard to recollect. Images have been saved, and words, but they're isolated; it's the interlinkage of what I've rescued that I lose. Perhaps a full chronologic narrative would show a crime and me to be guilty, so I've had reason to forget. I'd chance one now. But years have enshrouded the data and I have waited too long; and anyway, even were I the criminal, the pain of the little I do remember has been payment enough.

I suspect that the weeks were humdrum, *happy* as such. I'd divined the meaning of happiness in the war: mere life led. No one could feel the suck of the vortex—unless it was Ingeborg, and knowing made her silent. She spoke worried but once, I recall. Jake had been *downstairs*, had seen, and wasn't talking to Selma. *Let's just hope there isn't worse*, she said, staring through the walls in a fright, and I thought of her unvoiced plea when I'd left the prayer-session. If Ingeborg knew and was brooding, she gave no more evidence of it. Jake must not have been too disturbed; his remote good manners didn't change, and soon he was recognizing Selma. The idyll abetted him and so did our naivete. He had leisure in which to prepare the next act. I did ask Ben to keep an eye out for rooms. Had I inquired myself, there would have been gossip I didn't want the Revlands to hear. My brother, the nonpareil of discretion, said yes immediately (no need to tell him the why) and I was sure he'd do the job in confidence. I got a report in three days. *How about the old Moe cottage? Buy or rent, you'd have that cheap.* Yes, I'd remarked it in passing and liked it, but I was distracted; he had a cast on his thumb. There'd been a spell of warmth in the icy fall and he had decided to ventilate. In the afternoon—it was November and the chill would rise with the sun's setting—he'd gone to close up and the sash of the big east window had nailed him. Ben was ruing his own carelessness and said Doc had charged too much, but he must have been even madder than he seemed: not a window has been opened since 1921. I'd chuckle, were I disremembering. That thumb was to mean a lot. When I was shut in my sorrow and drunk and he brought me food, I saw the cast, not him, and I prayed for the bone's mending; I didn't care about mine; when the cast came off my drinking slowed and in a week I was out of bed. The thumb would never be the same, nor I, yet both would do.

A bereft man usually remembers, in detail, the end of the time preceding *it*. Relatives surround him with commiseration, allowing him to rave and cry—*it was just last night that she!*—and so to place the event in the almanac of what is supposed to occur because it does. Mourning to myself, I didn't find the lines; there's nowhere I could look it up and read and be consoled. On our last afternoon we drove to Moorhead, and I could prove as much. The recital had been announced in *The Fargo Express*: P. Fremstad, violinist, Concordia College, November 20, 1921. All I'd have to do is ask a librarian. I burnt our copy of the program but I know I could search out another. The performance was well-attended, the artist a hit. That afternoon came on a Sunday. Fremstad would have been written of in the Monday or Tuesday issue of the *Express*, and in one of those pages would be mention of Ingeborg. But my own record of the afternoon of November 20, 1921 is inadequate. I think we had invited Art and Tina to go along and they couldn't; Tina's sister in Nora was about to have a baby and wanted her help; and then Selma and Jake, who also declined. I remember crossing the Nora bridge—we always took the Minnesota route to the cities—and Ingeborg noticing the ice on the Red. *We should get our skates out*, I can hear her saying. *No, it won't be solid till next month* was the reply; or do I only wish it had been? But the ice looked thick, no snow dulling its surface. How Ingeborg seemed, I have lost. Fremstad played in an upstairs auditorium and he was short and dark and lived up to his epithet, *virtuoso of virtuosi*, and the people demanded two encores, nobody applauding harder than O. H. Iverson who had finagled a seat in the *orchestra*. I can name just one of the selections: the violin concerto of Jan Sibelius. Fremstad had but a pianist accompanying him, but those two short men were equal to the size of the music. It was because of a theme, the second theme in the first movement, that I could identify the concerto. That's what I sang on the drive back as I sipped Doc Benson's hooch. Yes, the liquor: of all the kinds available, Doc's was the best; he understood chemistry. Had I purchased it for the outing? Ingeborg tried some, I think, and she may have told me to watch the road. Hooch was part of the vortex and I drank it both in and out. Why my glimpse of O. H. survived the spin, I don't know. He hadn't seen *us*, and later, when he spoke of *the great Per Fremsta who came in tventy-vun*, he wasn't trying to hurt me; I've liked him the more for having been present in our *stretto*. But I remember much of the evening, a time the liquor conserved.

I was rattling drunk when we got to the farm, Ingeborg just a bit. *Now hush*, she kept saying as we swayed hand in hand through the yard, *we're going to have to eat with them, so hush.* I'm drunk enough tonight to recover the spirit of the scene that followed and catch what an abstinent review would miss, the import of its crazy-sounding dialogue; I've become daring; but there isn't enough liquor in the world to ease the pang of it. I was bold then too. Selma advised us to wait and eat in an hour or so, *when he's in bed*, and I smiled and patted her arm and went rejoicing on in the direction of the set table. Even had she locked the door, I would have taken no heed. I'd have supped with the Red Army that night.

Again it was the dining room table, a show of china and silver and cloth. The air was tense, no doubt, Jake having readied it; but I just got the impressions and not the warning in them.

It smells like snow out there, I said, grabbing a seat.

There was no wine. I saw, however, that Jake and I were of the same party. He noted it also and was quick to change tactics: *You must have enjoyed the concert?*

I had, but my mind was stuck on the weather. *If it warms up like this the snow is coming. Hope there isn't a blizzard.*

The women were in their places. *Ya, they forecast a little*, said Selma. *Help yourselves now,*

Papa was asking about the recital. Ingeborg looked as though she'd been told something odious.

But Jake seemed happy to accept a change of subject as well. His expression was a good innkeeper's. *We could use some*, he said. *Do you suppose it might rain first?*

That was great violin-playing — he did a whole concerto! You and the missus should have been there.

The bowls went round, localizing our attention. I had two objectives: to stuff myself; and to sing the theme for those who hadn't heard it.

What did you say his name was?

Sibelius! He's a Swede or Finnish, I think.

Oh, Villy, said Ingeborg, *he meant the performer.*

Jake winked at Selma. *Our son-in-law has trouble with names. What*

can we expect? He won't even say his own. It was Sibelius gave the concert — Sibelius? That's odd. The newspaper had it wrong, evidently.

My mistake, I said, pretending to be embarrassed. *Fremstad was the name of the violinist. I got him mixed up with the composer.*

He laughed to indicate that he was teasing. *It's not important. You've had a long day, and music can remove one's thoughts from the netherworld we live in. You're still above the clouds. When you're prepared to descend and talk our language, let us know. Would you?*

In 1941, Stalin and Hitler were to exchange sweet glances over Poland. So Jake eyed Villy and Villy him, our Poland the table. We couldn't stop smiling; if one of us did, someone would attack. I had a third objective now and meeting it would require all the patience I'd been taught: to strike, but not until I was ready.

The lull disquieted Ingeborg, who got up and asked me to come into the next room. I met her in the kitchen and saw that she was biting her lip. *This is no good*, she whispered. *I don't even want to eat, the way it's going. Mama says he went out and bought some and he's hidden it. Couldn't we eat later, Villy — please? Papa's about to get obnoxious, I can just tell, and I don't want to hear him. I don't have the strength.*

But I was unreachable. *Nonsense. We can eat here. It's our home too, isn't it? Wait if you wish, but I intend to have my supper.*

Jake was still smiling as we returned; he hadn't touched his fork. *May we begin?*

Sorry, I said. Ingeborg had angered me and it was hard to smile back.

You're sorry? Why? You've disrupted a meal before, haven't you? You weren't sorry then. It almost seems you find our company unpleasant. I hope this isn't so; we happen to enjoy yours. It's true, Mr. — Mr. No Name. In spite of what you think of us, we enjoy your company. I was on the verge of complimenting you when you left. Mrs. Revland and I are proud to have a son-in-law with a taste for serious music; so I would have said. Other young people may go to dances and listen to cheap songs, but you like good music. You like the music of tradition. I was on the verge of saying that you have a rare personality, and then you left — so perhaps you don't even care for the traditional.

Oh, but I do, I said, eating. I'd play along with him but I wouldn't fast.

Jake dropped the smile, assumed an innocuous, catlike expression and relaxed. He thought he'd be the only pouncer. *Then I was right: you do respect the traditional, the heritage of the ages. And here I was beginning to doubt you. How could I? If you like the music of tradition, you also respect the traditions of society. I shoud have deduced it.*

Mr. Revland, are you planning to eat? Selma sat haggard, looking at no one.

Of course! he made a poison-treacle face. *I'm not one to ask that a blessing be said, and I love to jump up and leave when others are waiting—unlike our custom-bound son-in-law. I abhor tradition. So you'll have to excuse my uncouth ways. Let's have some fodder!*

He seized a handful of cooked carrots and tossed them onto his plate. Ordinarily, I'd have watched in mute amusement, but, drunk as I was, I laughed. Jake peered at me; this wasn't in the script. He knew it was *down* at him I had laughed, not to his homage, and that such an insult could not be ignored. Wiping his hand, Jake paused to think. Then he turned friendly and serious.

Now, to continue—revenge would be later: *you say that you respect the traditional. Good. Now: we see you in church and you're not a thief, so you must also respect the laws of tradition, and the mores. Am I right? Yes or no?*

Ya, I said, paying overmuch attention to the steak.

Well, most other young people are quite different. Not only do they steal, they shun the church of the ages. The times are against you. Why is it that you hold to tradition? Are you better than everyone else?

I haven't met the people you're describing.

I understand. You live in Hedmark Township, North Dakota, and you can't tell a pyrrhonist from a hog. But you must read the newspaper. You read of the concert there, didn't you?

Jake had used an unfamiliar word. I'd have to parry: *It was a recital, not a concert.*

He peered at me again, at Selma and Ingeborg, too, as though to assay the effect. They revealed nothing but listlessness. Go ahead and fight, their bowed heads seemed to say; we know it's inevitable. That must have assured him. *The doctor speaks*, he went on, his wrath still in ambush, *and the untaught listen. Thank you. A man of your knowledge should never have married into the peasantry. But you have, and you've chosen to sit at our table, and all I can do is ask that you tolerate our ignorance. Would you be so kind?*

He meant that I should salaam. I only shrugged.

But Jake overlooked me; he had his mind on the script and wouldn't stray from it now. *Yes, you are an upstanding young person. You don't lie, you don't steal, you don't philander, you don't dance. On the contrary, you go to church and you enjoy serious music and you respect traditional mores. How fortunate we are to have such a son-in-law. There's just one thing wrong.* He shook his head and tried to simulate moral anguish. *I know that you don't want to pray with us, but that isn't it. You don't want to give us your name and that isn't it either. We've learned to be humble. What I find troubling I'm almost shy to mention, it's so insignificant. Anyhow, I think I should put it before you. Now: when a young man wishes to marry, is it or is it not traditional that the young woman's father be asked?*

I felt the blood in my ears; he had drawn it. Don't let him know, I told myself. Be the stooge. The time isn't yet. *Under most circumstances —*

Yes or no.

Yes.

Jake took off his worry-mask. *Well, am I relieved! Somewhere I had gotten the idea that you'd say no, it's not traditional, the father doesn't count. I had underestimated the depth of your traditionalism. Odd of me, wasn't it? A man must live by his convictions. I should have had an eye to your own example.*

I don't follow you, I said, showing him bait.

He swallowed it at once, and eagerly, but his tone became didactic. *Oh? That's surprising. I'll reduce it to the simplest terms, which even you will comprehend — all right? Now: mores are the customs of society. As such, they are traditional. You are a traditionalist. So you must hold mores in respect. Courtship is guided by mores. As a traditionalist, then, you'd naturally adhere to mores when you went courting. Are you with us?*

Selma began a half-hearted rebuke: *What does it matter, all that old —*

I couldn't hear the rest. *Villy, I'm tired*, my wife broke in.

You sit till I'm finished, I said, unseeing, too much in character to be a husband. How did she look?

Meanwhile, the first shout had gone up. It was Jake at Selma: *—is way beyond you!*

Our women quelled, Jake and I could return to important business. *Now—* he seemed happy at the point his shouting had brought him to*—you may answer. Why the ladies interrupted I really can't say. I'd* *have thought the subject would be of interest to them. But, since they did, I'll repeat the question: when a young man goes courting, is it traditional or is it not that he ask the young woman's father? All right?*

I've already answered that.

I had abashed him, the master of the seamless argument; his gaze went traveling, then inward. An alcoholic hates to be reminded. He didn't stew for long, though. *Ladies, you mustn't interrupt again*, he said with a smirk of dismissal, *and you, sir, should be more attentive. Have you lost your hearing? The question was this: if you were a man who wished to marry—follow?—if you were a young man who wished to get married, would you respect traditional mores to the extent of asking the young woman's father?*

The china was gold-rimmed, the glasses too, and every piece bore the same involved rosette. The design meant nothing but it absorbed me, in particular the one on my glass. What I saw, no doubt, was an emblem of the vortex. Jake got most of my attention, however; and had I been able to solve the rosette, I could not have said *Ya* to him.

Ya? Ya, he answers? The table shook slightly. He was preparing to give it a Thor's blow. I studied the design. *Whose language does he talk? I think we have a rustic here. Ya? I hope it's not Yes you're saying. Because if it's Yes—ah, then you're a liar. You've called yourself a liar!* Thor struck and the world trembled. Jake roared like a god, too. *You would ask the young woman's father, you say? Is that it? Look at yourself! Is that what you did? You came to this place—a bum, a tramp, a nobody!—but I treated you well and showed you all the riches and dreams I have, and you had a hundred opportunities to do the right thing, to ask for my daughter's hand in marriage! And you wouldn't do it! But we took you in anyway—we're Christians, you know! We thought we could civilize you, and how did you respond? Why, you wouldn't even tell us your name! Poking fun at my dead mother, that was all right, that you could do; and now you sit and toy with us and correct us and pretend to be a supporter of traditional mores, something the likes of you are unworthy to speak of! You're not even worthy of that glass you're holding! And you say you asked me for Ingeborg's hand? Yes, you say? I think you have some explaining to do, and I suggest you make it good! I don't want a liar in this house!*

Slowly, I turned the glass; when the design reappeared I spoke. *I said I would have.*

No, then? It was my refusal to anger, not my words, that had Jake foaming. He couldn't see. *You admit it? How very brave! It won't work, young man! Do you know where you've left yourself? If you say you didn't do what you believe you should have done, then you're worse than I thought—worse than a liar! You're a hypocrite!*

Jake saw my calm. He couldn't see through it. *You may be right*, I said, *but there's something worse than a hypocrite. It's a drunk who likes to fondle his daughter.*

With this I stared at him, grinning. He pushed away from the table, mouth shocked open, eyes quick, head wheeling as he searched for an insult, or an object, to throw; but soon his teeth met on the only words that could recoup him. *That's it!* He had to spit them out. *You! You! Leave this house at once!*

The automaton I had become got up—not I, it was the fury's puppet—and took the glass and went to him and heaved the water in his face. The battle was short. He jumped for me and I struck and watched him go, and I remember voices (Ingeborg's yelling, *You've hurt Papa!*) and the sight of Jake downed but moving, Selma inspecting him (*Oh he'll live!*), and Ingeborg pulling my sleeve as I marched to the kitchen (*Villy, you've got to stay!*) to fetch my cap and coat and gloves, and telling her *It isn't my choice*, and the last thing she ever said to me (*Where do I belong?*), and stepping on out to the dark; but I was too inhuman, too automatic, to *live* the moment, and I can't remember pain I haven't felt. Better to have cursed or even hit Ingeborg than to have denied her all warmth, I know. It was warmth she ran in search of, not me, and she didn't find it. I had retreated to my past, to Hedmark, getting there as soon as I'd left the Revlands'; the puppet I had become was unable to recall the walking.

The road from Hedmark to Nora is straight, and the bridge nearer Nora, until just north of that town, where it curves right with a half mile to go. A mile east of Hedmark and one north sits the Revland (today, the Johannesson) farm; someone walking the fields between there and Hedmark has only about a mile to cover. That was my route in the evening of November 20, 1921. When I arrived I had snow on my coat and Ben was in bed and coughed to greet me. *I've got to stay here*, I informed him, and he said nothing as I lurched to my old celibate room and undressed and tried to sleep. It was an hour, though, before I could put Jake out of my thoughts and did.

Hedmark to Nora is a three-mile drive; Revlands' to Nora the same. In an average winter, the Red being crossable, one could walk direct from the Revlands to Nora and trim the distance—could but wouldn't: he'd ski. When there's so little snow that one can walk, why not drive? The winter of '21, beginning cold and snowless, had turned the plowed fields to granite. It wasn't average. But the Red had seemed solid. If I had a map and drew a line from Revlands' to Nora, that line would pass through the Lindgren farmstead.

Ben woke me much too soon. There was dawn in the windows, not my head. Strange he'd come visiting us so early, I half-thought; must be trouble. He stood inside the doorway, a mug in his left hand. The right had the cast. Straining to hear him made me realize where we were.

You've got a phone call.

Oh? Ingeborg?

It's your mother-in-law. She wanted to talk to Ingeborg first. What's the deal?

To talk to Ingeborg? Eight it was by the switchboard clock. The morning would be sunny, harsh; about an inch of snow lay loose on the ground. I felt sick. There had been times like this in Russia—bombardment at sunrise, premature waking, anemia—and I hoped Selma would put an end to it.

But no, she couldn't help. *You mean she isn't with you? Where in the world—and she's not in town? I can't imagine. Maybe she went to Tina's.*

Ingeborg's not at home? I said, fearing the fear in Selma's voice.

She took her things and ran out last night, an hour after you left, must have been. The snowing had stopped. I thought she had gone to you. This is terrible, Villy. It's her health; she's never been strong. Guess I'll have to call Tina.

Ingeborg had run out and not to me, had taken *her things*. I didn't understand. *Yes, you do that*, I said. *I'll drive over and—to the front of your place, on the road. See you in a couple of minutes.*

I told my brother's questioning face that I had to use the truck, and, if Ingeborg called, *have her meet me here*. Then I was driving through the new winter, the land, as in Russia, smug and blank, its message Come die in me, and even before I saw Selma, I must have remembered. She stood at the edge of the grove, a diminutive figure in a white scarf, and when I slowed, she trotted up crying. Tina had been in Nora. I must have known.

—where her sister lives, the one that married the Askegaard boy and

who's having a baby, so Tina's been with them to assist. Selma leaned against the door of the truck, and I sat nodding. *But I called the Askegaards' and talked to Tina and no, she says, they haven't seen Ingeborg either, and I was going to call Pete but you were on the way so I hurried out. It's terrible. Just look.*

Selma pointed. A set of footprints led southeast, clear in the immaculate snow. Already I was buttoning my coat to the chin.

To run off like this, and in the dark! but she was no longer crying. *Well, she might have gone to Pete's.*

Ask him, why don't you, and some others. I'll be back.

I parked and got out in the chill morning. Yes, her tracks led straight southeast, following a line that would meet the distant riverwoods at a spot above and beyond which rose the tip of the spire of the Nora Lutheran, and the sun was climbing a few degrees over to the north of that. Yes, Ingeborg had been running, stumbling here and there too; the plowed earth was hard but jagged and the snow masked it, and by night it would have been tough to cross. I began at a walk. The line would also intersect the Hedmark-Nora road, where perhaps I'd see she'd turned left and toward the Johannesson farm by the bridge; an encouraging thought and it wouldn't last. The footprints continued on the other side. I was angry with Ingeborg now and ran, rehearsing all that I'd say when I caught her. Why had she gone this way and not to me? We could have talked—we should have. She'd deserted the man she was married to, the bitch! I raced and raged along, the wirelike trees bobbing closer, then a wall of the Lindgren house. Ingeborg had to be in it; she *took her things*. There had to be smoke in the chimney.

No, she'd passed through the yard—hadn't even seen the home our love was building—and into the meadow. Did I spare it a glance myself or chase on by? Tonight, remembering, I seem to have slackened there. A good huntsman can tell when the quarry's lost. I stuck to the trail, but the rush and rage were over. The pastureland lay white before me, Grandma's canvas; upon it she'd brush a Swedish meadow with *lone oaks and everything* but no people in sight. It was November 21st and so much the color of the whit she had been. I seem to have prayed as I walked. Praying is not ecclesiastical. In prayer one talks to *everything*, within and out, and I think I prayed both for and to my Ingeborg, Sibelius' theme shrilling in my head. *Where do I belong?* she'd asked, and our lives' conversation broke off. It changed to prayer and in time to this: the search in words of a man of fifty-three. I haven't given up, *but I'm done hoping. Tonight I must reach you, or whatever of you in the world remains. Some of you saw the end of my morning trek. In the trees beyond the pastureland it was hushed; rabbits and foxes had marked the snow and vanished, and only woodpeckers were about. You'd tripped on a half-sunk log and bushes had clawed you. There was a hole where an uprooted elm had stood. You had pitched into it, leaving a sketch of yourself on the ground. It must have been hard going, the night moonless, and your trail was crooked now; but always you got up or went back to it and ran on, as though tugged by your destiny. Had you guessed its name? I had. Coming after it had happened, I knew, and I needn't tell: you would have heard the praying that began in the woods, the sorrowing, the river still ahead. Forgive, forgive, forgive, was all I could say. The bank was gentle with a short drop at its foot. You had jumped, and the solidity of the ice had emboldened you—did you think of my warning?—and the rest of the story was patent. The thin midstream ice had broken for you. One set of footprints led to the crack (and the opening was larger than what you would have made, the snow yellowing around it), none returned, none emerged. I sank to my knees. The theme wouldn't quit nor the woodpeckers' drumming. I should have joined you in the music but I was the coward of terra firma and you had gone, those prints your last vestige in the barnyard of existence. You were never found; found, as the law would have it. I don't have to repeat all this. You were there when your uncle arrived and looked at the story and at me and said, No, my God. Then: We're too late; let's go notify the sheriff. Selma had talked to him and he'd seen me in the field. I went back with him, a mute coward, and sat in the house while he called Wahpeton and Selma, but I didn't want to wait for the sheriff's crew and Pete understood. He gave me a ride to the truck. Perhaps you had written a note, I was thinking; it seemed to have been more deliberate than accidental. I couldn't go into your folks', however, I just couldn't, and I thanked him and was able to say that I'd be in Hedmark. He said, I'll let them know; take it easy. But they never found you. They broke up the ice and dragged and dragged, and in the spring they tried again. Musta drifted way north, they concluded, or got snagged on something. Ben and Selma saw to the funeral, and I was brought there drunk to ignore the sermon and the sympathetic words of the township. Your casket was empty. You left nothing to the boneyard of existence either. How could we bury you? How could I visit the grave? You weren't in it. I have yet to read the stone. You knew all that and all that ensued, the drinking, the praying, the slow resurrection (and at Christmas you even came to me, in the warmth of Tina's apple pie), you've known it through the years, and I repeat it only because I have to reach you. I want you to hear me. When you went, I should have followed, but it was for you I stayed, keeping to the land of which you're the essence, living as you'd have me do and almost as we might have done, yet hiding from the whole of you till now; and I must tell you it's over. I can accept you in everything you inhabit, Ingeborg. The afterlife is part of the barns and bones of this existence. You are where you belonged.*

I'd mistold Selma; I never went back to the Revlands'. Throughout the nine or so years Jake had to live, Fargo Bell handled the servicing there. It must have cost. Avoiding the man I hated was easy. The township is inward, its public life as clock-directed as its private; I knew who'd be where and when. Church would have been a risk. But I had ceased going, and not only on their account. Tiseth and the congregation had celebrated my loss, I felt, or had sought to dupe me. Moreover, Jake's ranting had ruined all God-talk. It was his worship of death, revived in common each Sunday, that had sent her into the night. I would pray alone. Nor did I see Selma. A month after the mimic-burial, at New Year's, she packed up our *things* and had them delivered and she also wrote. *Let's you and I not blame ourselves too much. This accident that has taken a daughter and a wife is of the Lord's doing and even in sorrow and bitterness we must trust Him. Villy, try to be charitable in your thoughts of Mr. Revland. He did ill and is suffering more than you know. Try to pardon the sin though he doesn't ask, and me who have vowed to be at his side. I hope that one day I'll see you again* and what did he put Ingeborg through, I fumed, that night when I had left? I ripped the letter and junked the *things*, burning all I could. He was another getting his hooch from Doc, starting, probably, November 20th; Ben with his exigent thumb had learned of it. I never replied or went back or saw Selma. Tina used to hint, but no. If I was manning the switchboard and Selma came on the line, I'd treat it as just another call. I had told Selma wrong and have done it too. Tomorrow I'll write.

This talking and sniveling must have wakened Ben. He groans to indicate the hour, two or three, I'd say. Perhaps he was dreaming of his own loss, Tina. Yet a certain Tina, the girl of thirty-five years ago, will always belong to him as Ingeborg does to me. Young Ben would not have recognized the living Mrs. Engstrom I saw on the road this afternoon, or not without effort. Would I know Ingeborg?

So much of what we've been looks unfamiliar to us. But I think we *are* the vestiges we leave, a conglomerate of all we've made. We have the intellect to be the synthesis but we use it for more divarication. My walking, doing self is just an agent for what I am. Ingeborg's Villy is waiting in the Lindgren house. When I go there in the morning, I'll try to recognize the abandoned work — and him, the vestige I have feared. I'll be as close to Ingeborg as he was.

The alcohol's worn off and I should let Ben sleep and sleep myself. He's good. I won't quit him or the company. But I want to move, buy the Lindgrens' and loaf in the lap of nature so that I'll be set to join the *everything*; I want it now. He'll understand. He's felt it too, the impulse that would keep us hunting the vestiges we've left, and knows the true direction of the path. It seems to lead away but takes us round and home. It's the *élan vital* we serve. What more can be expected of us? Death will do the synthesizing.

NEW RIVERS PRESS

— presents —

Title: VILLY SADNESS (A Novella)

Author: RODNEY NELSON

Graphics: Cover and Inside Drawings by
        TRYGVE OLSON

PUBLICATION DATE: 31 October 1987

PRICE: $7.95 (paperback only)

PAGES: 113

ISBN: 0-89823-093-4

L of C NUMBER: 86-63567

We are pleased to send you this book for review. We would appreciate receiving two copies of any notice you give it.

New Rivers Press
1602 Selby Avenue
St. Paul, Minnesota
55104

(612) 645-6324

Publicity: Susan Bergholz
(212) 799-6973

Distribution:
The Talman Company
(212) 620-3182